A Selection of Poetry Works:
MY TEARS FLOW ENDLESSLY
Forced Out of House and Home by the Fukushima Nuclear Power Accident
Kojima Chikara, Noda Setsuko

詩集 わが涙滂々(抄)──原発にふるさとを追われて
小島 力[著] 野田説子[英訳]

西田書店 Nishidashoten publishing

A Selection of Poetry Works:

MY TEARS FLOW ENDLESSLY

Forced Out of House and Home

by the Fukushima Nuclear Power Accident

詩集
わが涙滂々〈抄〉
原発にふるさとを追われて

Forced Out of House and Home by the Fukushima Nuclear Power Accident
CONTENTS

In the Midst of the Earthquake and the Tsunami 6

The Morning I Couldn't Go Home
——At the Municipal Apartment Complex in Musashino City 10

Longing for Home 14

Killer 18

A Story about Shiro 22

A Demonstration of Five 26

Returning Home Temporarily
  After One Year and Four Months 30

  Infiltration 30

  Nobody Knows 32   Rampant Weeds 34

  I Took It for Granted 36

  Silent Village 40

  Going to Sleep 42

  Kashi, Kashi (Half Dead, Half Dead) 44

From My Works Three Decades Ago

Workers for Sub-Contractors at a Nuclear Power Plant 50

Adding to the Ant Tower 58

An Epitaph 66

Autumn Castle Fortress　74

Nuclear Power Plant: A Dialogue　80

I Can Hear　88

Fires　94

Epilogue: War, Nuclear Power and My Work　102

Translator's Afterword　116

目　　次

原発にふるさとを追われて

地震・津波のさ中で　7
帰れない朝
　──武蔵野市・都営アパートで──　11
望　郷　15
殺し屋　19
シロの話　23
五人のデモ隊　27
一年四か月目の一時帰宅　31
　潜入　31　誰も知らない　33　草
　茫々　35　当たり前の　37　沈黙の
　村　41　寝る　43　仮死々々　45

三十年前の作品から

原発下請労働者　51
蟻たちの塔に寄せて　59
聞き書きの墓碑銘　67
秋の城　75
原発問答　81
聴こえる　89
火　災　95

来歴・三題
　──あとがきに代えて──　103
訳者あとがき　117

Forced Out of House and Home
by the Fukushima Nuclear Power Accident

原発にふるさとを追われて

In the Midst of the Earthquake and the Tsunami

With a mountainous roar
The first shock wave hit.
Then came the vertical tremor
Like a huge iron hammer had struck the ground.
The tremors became stronger and stronger
As I got out of my computer room, heading to my living room
Through two 8-*tatami* mat rooms.

The crashing dishes echoed from the kitchen
And our dog barked madly.
Just past our front yard,
The ground bounced our little car up and down like a ball.
Yet I did not ask myself,
"What about the nuclear power plants?"

The earthquake did not cease for almost two hours,
Sometimes stronger, sometimes weaker.
The TV, which we kept on during the earthquake,
Was broadcasting the tsunami on the coast of
Tohoku again and again on the screen.
Amazed at the tremendous height of the furious tsunami,
I still did not come up with the question,
"What about the nuclear power plants?"

地震・津波のさ中で

底ひびきする山鳴りと同時に
第一波の衝撃
更に続けざま巨大な鉄槌を
大地に叩きつけるような縦揺れ
パソコン室から八畳の部屋二つを通り越し
居間に出てくるその間も
揺れがますます激しくなった

炊事場で食器の砕け散る音がひびき
犬がけたたましく吠える
庭先の軽自動車が軽々と跳ね上がり
ボールのように地面で弾んでいる
しかしその時まだ
「原発が？」とは気づきもしなかった

大地の震動は強まったり弱まったり
二時間近くも揺れ止まなかった
点けっぱなしのテレビが東北沿岸の
津波の映像を繰り返し放送している
巨大な水の猛威に目を見張りながら
「原発は？」とはまだ思い及ばなかった

For over 40 years,
I have fought against nuclear power.
Yet the nuclear power plants did not occur to me
In the midst of the earthquake and tsunami
Until the TV news started to report
The collapse of a nuclear power plant…

That's why even to this day,
I sometimes resent acutely that
I could not ask the question;
My heart feels like
A rusted nail has lodged deep inside.

過去四十数年
原発反対で押し通してきた筈の私が
地震・津波のそのさ中
原発を思い起こすことは
ついになかった
テレビが原発の破綻を伝え始める
その時まで………

だから今でも
心の奥底の深い暗がりで
その事実が執拗に突き刺さり
時折　錆びついた古釘のように
疼き始めるのだ

The Morning I Couldn't Go Home
——At the Municipal Apartment Complex in Musashino City

In bed, in a half-awake doze,
I'm wondering if I'd better pile soil around the potato sprouts
To protect them from frost, or harvest young green peas
Drenched with morning dew.
These were my usual morning rituals
When I was at home in Fukushima, where
I may never return.
Yet, in my half-asleep state,
I'm still feeling in the dark for morning in Fukushima,
Though it fades away day by day, and
The touch of a borrowed *futon* blanket
Tells me this is not my home.

I stand on the balcony of my temporary residence
In the municipal apartment complex and
I see that today has weak sunlight, high clouds again.
The noise of the big city can be heard
Through the fresh green of roadside ginkgo trees,
Like the sound of waves from afar.
My day starts in this still unfamiliar town,
Pressing forward as quickly as the second hand of my watch.

帰れない朝
　　——武蔵野市・都営アパートで——

まだ覚めやらぬうつつの中で
今朝は伸び始めたじゃが薯の芽に
霜除けの土寄せをしようか
しとゞに朝露を浴びた
さやえんどうの緑を摘もうかと
もしかしたらもう帰れないかもしれない
福島の日常をまさぐっている
次第に目覚めてゆく知覚が
仮の住まいの支給された布団の
感触を伝えているのに
日々遠のいてゆく福島の朝を
まだ手さぐりしている

都営住宅のヴェランダに立てば
団地の空は
今日も薄日の高曇り
新緑の銀杏並木の梢を越えて
遠い潮騒のような都会の朝の騒音が
伝わってくるので
まだ住み慣れない町の暮らしが
速すぎる秒針みたいに
進み始める

On that day,
We, residents were forced out
From villages hugging the *Abukuma* mountains
And from towns crouched round the nuclear power plant.
We were all flicked away
Like rain drops from a windshield.
On that dark night,
All I remember is that we were searching
For shelters from place to place
In fear of something invisible.

So that's where it stands.
I may never return to morning in Fukushima.
Everything in my homeland–
Trees, grass, roads, paddies and fields, –is contaminated
With cesium and iodine caked on like frost.
My home village is occupied, violated
By an ugly force, called radioactivity.

阿武隈の山ひだにへばりついた村々や
原発の足元にうずくまる町々が
ワイパーで水滴をはじき飛ばすように
たった一晩でリセットされた
あの日
眼に見えない恐怖に追われた
避難先たらいまわしの
暗夜の記憶

だからもう
決して帰れないかもしれない
福島の朝は
草木にも道にも田畑にも
ふるさとの風物のすべてに
セシウムやヨウ素が
霜のようにびっしりと凍りつき
放射能と言う醜悪な武力で
占拠され　蹂躙された
ふるさとである

Longing for Home

I'd like to go back home, but I can't
Because invisible materials pile up
Silently on my homeland.
Nobody can work out what this evil spirit is,
Especially not the group of evacuees
Deposited at the shelter.

Radioactivity spread from the explosions March 12th to 15th.
It has settled in several towns and villages in the *Futaba* district.
As minute particles of dust and fine ashe scattered around
And accumulated on plants, birds, and animals,
The innocent locals were all driven away;
Deserted houses remain in ruins.

I'd like to go back home, but I can't
Because my homeland is full of colorless,
Tasteless, odorless material
Diffusing and floating in the air.
Only when I go back home for a short time
Can I see mountains and rivers as before
Against the sky above the *Abukuma* Highlands.

What the merciless, indiscriminate radioactivity
Has taken from us, the inhabitants of the Futaba district

望　郷

　　　　帰りたい　でも帰れない
　　　まだ帰れない　ふるさとの大地に
　　　　音もなく降り積むものは
人目には決して見えない物質だから
集団で避難先に運ばれた人々も
　　　襲いかかった魔物の正体を
まだ誰も突き止めてはいない

3.12〜15爆発で飛散した放射能が
　　　双葉地方の町や村に居すわり
　　　　微細な塵や灰を撒き散らし
草木や鳥や獣に蓄積されるので
罪もない住民は根こそぎ追い払われ
　　　　人気の途絶えた家々が
　　　廃墟となって立ち並ぶのだ

　　　　戻りたい　でも戻れない
　　　まだ戻れない　ふるさとの大気に
　　　　拡散し　浮遊するものは
色も形も匂いもない物質だから
一時帰宅の目に映る山や川は
　　　　阿武隈の空の下に
いつもと同じ顔で広がっている

　　　理不尽に降りかかる放射能が
双葉地方の住民から奪い去ったものは

Are homes and lands where we were born and raised.
Those who were exiled from home so brashly
Must go on wandering aimlessly
Under the skies of other lands.

I'd like to go back home, but I can't.
I'd like to go back home, even if it's not an option.
Although my homeland is infringed upon by invisible impurity,
I'd like to go back as long as
There is my home and my fields.
Yet all I can do is to commit to return home
Eventually, someday.

　　　　生まれ育ったふるさと
　　　　我が家とわが土地だから
　　いとも無造作に放逐された人々は
　　　　　　　　異郷の空の下で
　　あてもなくさすらい続けるのだ

　　　　　　だからこそ帰りたい
　　　　　　帰れないふるさとへ
　　　　帰れなくとも　帰りたい
　目に見えぬ穢れに侵された土地でも
　　我が家と田畑が　そこにある限り
　　　帰りたい　いつか必ず帰ると
　　　　　　　　決意するしかないのだ

Killer

The real killer in this society
   is probably hidden and raised secretly
     under a veil of radio waves, letters and words.
The real killer without color, shape or smell,
   can be seen by nobody.

The real killer, who targets every creature on earth,
   doesn't discriminate targets.
The real killer, who itself is the lethal weapon,
   has no need for any hidden weapon.
The real killer, who intrudes on and accumulates in the body,
   can never be eradicated, though reduced by half.
The real killer, who makes sure to do its work and take its time,
   always gets its way
     even if people remain unaware.

The real killer never had a passport
   enabling it to stay anywhere on earth;
The real killer, who crosses the border to the northwest,
   does not restrict itself to the designated concentric circle.
The real killer, who tries to escape and expand to oceans——
   we cannot interrupt its attempt at world domination.
The real killer, who fashions false information into "myth"——
   truth must hide itself, wandering around in a ski mask,

殺し屋

　　　　本物の殺し屋は　この社会では
　　　　電波や文字や言葉のベールの陰で
　　　　多分　こっそりと飼育されている
　　本物の殺し屋は　色も形も匂いもないので
　　　　　人目には決して触れない

　　本物の殺し屋は　地表の生物すべてが獲物であり
　　　　　　　　ターゲットを特定しない
　　本物の殺し屋は　本人そのものが凶器であるから
　　　　　　　物々しい武器は隠し持たない
　　本物の殺し屋は　体内に侵入して蓄積するので
　　　　　半減はしても消去するプログラムがない
　本物の殺し屋は　じっくりとそして確実に作業するので
　　　　　人が忘れた頃にしか凶行に及ばない

　　　本物の殺し屋は　元々地球に滞在すべき
　　　　　　　　パスポートを持たない
　本物の殺し屋は　北西に舌を伸ばして越境するので
　　　　　同心円の内側に定住するとは限らない
　　本物の殺し屋は　脱出して海洋侵攻を企てるから
　　　　　世界制覇をくいとめる手立てがない
　本物の殺し屋は　偽りの情報を「神話」に仕立て上げるので
　　　真実は風評の目出し帽で徘徊するしかない

ashamed of the rumors.

The real killer, who will still remain even after reduced to ashes——
   there is no ideal grave for it,
The real killer, who seems dead at low temperatures,
   fights on though "in a state of apparent death"
   and can never be eradicated.
The real killer, who conceals itself in a village full of money,
   cannot be arrested even if its crime is discovered.
The real killer, who is dispersed in unexpected places——
   no creatures but loaches can live in contaminated soils.

The real killer, they tell us,
   "Doesn't affect your health immediately."
The real killer is, therefore, in this society
   most probably,
   without a doubt,
   legal.

本物の殺し屋は　コツになっても殺し屋は殺し屋であり
溜まった燃え殻の置き場がない
本物の殺し屋は　冷温停止に「状態」の下駄を履かせるから
しぶとく生き残ってトドメを刺せない
本物の殺し屋は　札束に囲われたムラに潜伏するので
犯行が露見してもみだりに逮捕されない
本物の殺し屋は　想定の外に拡散するので
汚染された土壌には泥鰌しか住めない

本物の殺し屋は　いつも決まって
「ただちに健康に影響はない」
本物の殺し屋は　だから　この社会では
多分　間違いなく
合法である

A Story about *Shiro*

Shiro is what you call a cluster of mushrooms in the wild.
Not even parents and children ever tell each other
The secret place of their *shiro* on their death bed.
Recently, people have come looking for mushrooms.
Many *shiro* are picked—now it's first come, first served.

On the continuous ridge, about 2.5 kilometers long,
There is a little peak halfway.
About 100 meters below the peak,
Is another small ridge, whose western side harbors my *shiro*.
My *shiro* is less than 1 hectare.
Over the decades since World War II
Nobody except me has ever found it.
When early mushrooms are too small,
I wait for the next rainfall.
I used to take as many mushrooms as I pleased——
So many that my backpack was full to the brim,
Using my jacket as a lid, and
I carried back two bags,
One in each hand, full of mushrooms.

Mushrooms——*shaka shimeji, hokidake, kurokawa,*
Shishidake, white *shimeji* and black *shimeji*.
When autumn comes,

シロの話

シロとは茸のシロである
親子の間でも教えないまま死ぬと言う
茸の秘密基地である
近年茸採り人口がやたらと増えて
誰もが競争で探しあさるので
多くのシロが早い者勝ちになった

二・五キロも続く長い尾根の
中ほどに小さなピークがあって
ピークから百メーターほど下った中腹から
新たに派生する小さな尾根があった
わずか一ヘクタールに満たない
その西向き斜面が私のシロである。
戦後数十年
誰一人そのシロに立ち入る者はなかった
出始めの茸が小さ過ぎたら
もう一雨降る時期を待って
山盛りの背負い篭に上着のフタを縛りつけ
両手に袋をぶら下げて帰ることもあった

釈迦シメジ　ほうき茸　クロカワ
しし茸　白シメジ　黒シメジ
移ろう季節を追いかけて

They grow one after another.
I used to send them to my children and grandchildren
As autumn gifts from the Abukuma Highlands.

Since the nuclear plant accident,
I've never again visited my *shiro*.
When autumn comes, the mushrooms grow.
I wonder if they will be rotten or dried up
With no one to harvest them.
Smothering the mountain side,
Falling leaves are nests of radioactivity.
My shiro is not mine anymore.
I cannot send gifts from my homeland
To my children and grandchildren who live in town.

茸は次々と頭を出した
阿武隈の秋の便りを
子供に送った
孫に送った

原発事故以来
一度もそのシロに行っていない
季節が来れば茸は律儀に顔を出し
誰にも採られることのない茸は
腐ったり干乾びたりするのであろうか
山の斜面を覆い尽くす落葉の堆積は
放射能の巣である
私のシロが私のシロではなくなった
町に住む子供たちにも孫たちにも
ふるさとの便りは
もう届かない

A Demonstration of Five

Mr. Oe[1] proclaimed, " Democracy is expressing your free will!"
Taro[2] declared "Save the Earth!"
Swarms of people in Meiji Park
With colorful banners, flags and balloons──
I've never been to a rally like this before,
A rally on 'free will.'

"You'd better go home
As soon as the rally finishes," my daughter said to me,
"There are too many people
To start a demonstration march on time.
Besides, the demonstration course is too long for you to walk."
I felt disappointed, but nodded,
"You can't beat old age. Rats!"

I said to myself, "This paper placard is useless after all."
Yesterday I spent all night making this placard:
In large letters, "I Oppose Nuclear Power " and
In small, "Society of Victims of Nuclear Power Plant Accidents."
It's still in my bag.

---

1 OE, Kenzaburo is a novelist; a Novel Prize winner in literature and is active in peace movement.
2 YAMAMOTO, Taro is an ex-actor and now a congressman after nuclear accident.

五人のデモ隊

「自分の意思を示すことが
民主主義だ」と大江さんが言った
「地球を守ろう」と太郎さんが叫んだ
人々々の明治公園
色とりどりの旗や幟やゴム風船
こんな集会に初めて出てきた
「自分の意思」で………

「集会が終わり次第
帰っていい」と娘が言った
「参加者があんまり多過ぎて
出発時間が遅れそうだし
デモのコースも長いから」と
「齢もトシだし　仕方がないか」
残念だけどもうなずいた

「タスキは結局無駄になったか」
心の隅でふと思った
百円ショップの障子紙折って
「脱原発」と大きく書いた
「原発被災者の会」と小さく書いた
ゆうべ一晩がかりで作った
タスキをバックに入れたままで

There are only five men in the victim society.
We began to walk to the station.
One of us said, "We went to the trouble to make them.
Why don't we show the placards while we walk?"
"You are right," the rest of us agreed.
We paused on the pedestrian path
To put on the placards on our shoulders.

"Democracy is expressing your free will!" Mr. Oe proclaimed.
Five elderly men slowly walked two kilometers
In a line, to the station.
With the afternoon sunshine on our backs,
We walked on cheerfully, faces bright,
Our backs radiant and glowing from behind.

「被災者の会」はたったの五人
駅に向かって歩き始めた
「折角作ったタスキだから
かけて歩こう」と誰かが言った
「そうだそうだ」と
みんなが応じた
歩道の片隅で肩から下げた

「自分の意思を示すことが
民主主義だ」と大江さんが言った
一列になって駅まで二キロ
熟年五人がゆっくり歩いた
午後の陽差しを背中に浴びて
みんなの顔が晴れやかになった
後ろ姿が輝いて見えた

Returning Home Temporarily
After One Year and Four Months

Infiltration

Before daybreak
We left the parking lot of our municipal apartment complex.
I'm a senior driver, over 70 years old,
So I used the Metropolitan Highway with my wife
Right after daybreak.
Ahead of us, there is a long way on the Tohoku Highway
To my home, too far away.

On March 12th, 2011
Right after the explosion,
We deserted our home
Fleeing in the direction
From which we are coming now.
Driving in the middle of the night on local streets.
We retreated about 290 kilometers, like losers.
The homeland we left behind
Is oppressed by the violence of radioactivity.
It's still trampled by it, unfairly,
Closed off by invisible barbed wire.
Our homeland is called a 'planned evacuation zone.'

一年四か月目の一時帰宅

潜入

　　　　　　　　　　夜明け前
　　　　　　都営住宅駐車場を出発する
　　　　　　七十過ぎた運転技術では
　　　　　　明け方直後の隙をついて
首都高速を抜け出す以外手はない
　　　　　　　その先にはかくも遠く
　　　ふるさとから隔てられた事実を
　　　　　　　　突きつけるかのように
東北道の長い行程が待ち受けている

　　　　　　　　　　2011年3月12日
　　　　　　　爆発と同時に脱出を企てた
　　　　　　　今行く方向を逆にたどり
　　　　　真夜中の一般道をひたすら
　　　　　　　　　　敗走二九〇キロ
　　　　　　　取り残されたふるさとは
　　　　放射能と言う武力に制圧され
　　　　　　　計画的避難区域と言う
目に見えない有刺鉄線にとり囲まれ
今も理不尽な蹂躙にさらされている

We crossed the county border
Where no guard with a carbine stands
And we sneaked onto our land and into our house.
Who occupied our homeland illegally?
Radioactivity? Or the nuclear power plant?
Yet the real enemies never revealed themselves
Only smiling impudently
Behind a wall of nuclear power money.

Nobody Knows

There are dozens of holes dug by wild boars,
In the farm in front of our house and in our garden.
Since the electric fences have been turned off,
They have intruded into the farm easily.
They live in the abandoned garden.

The earthworms live near the surface of the ground.
They live on soil and excrete it.
They make paddies and farms fertile.
Wild boars dig out farms and gardens to eat earthworms.
That's why both of them are said to have
The worst radiation poisoning, more than any other animals.

Wild boars and earthworms are unaware of
The nuclear power accident.
How does the radioactivity entering their bodies

カービン銃を構えた歩哨など
　　　いる筈もない郡境を越えて
　　わが土地と我が家に潜入する
　　　　　　　　このふるさとを
　　　　　　不法に占拠したのは誰？
　　　　　放射能？　それとも原発？
　いや　決して姿を表わさない敵は
原発マネーを積み重ねた壁の向こうで
　　　ふてぶてしくニンマリしている

　　　　　　　　　誰も知らない

　　　　　我が家のすぐ前の畑にも
　　　　　　　　庭の植木の間々も
　　　猪の掘り起こした穴だらけなのだ
　電気の切れた電気牧柵の線を押し切り
　猪が畑に入って掘り返し放題なのだ
　　　　　　　　　人の住まない庭先は
　　　　　彼らの格好の棲み家なのだ

　　　　　ミミズは地表近くに生息し
　　　　　　　　土を食い土を排泄し
　　　　田圃や畑を肥やすのだと言う
　　　　　　猪は畑や庭の土を掘り
　　　　　そのミミズを喰うのだと言う
　だから猪もミミズも他の動物より
　異常に放射線量が高いのだと言う

　　猪もミミズも原発事故を知らない

Undermine them gradually?
Will the earthworms come to the surface of the soil
And writhe in pain under the beating sun?
Will wild boars run around the mountains, maniacs
With their bristled back hair standing on end ?

Nobody knows.
Nobody sees.

Rampant Weeds

Rampant weeds
In fields and paddies.
A whole village in ruins with rampant weeds.

Two years ago,
Wind blew through the corn fields.
In fields of radishes, leaves were heavy with morning dew,
In those mountain fields,
Where we were content with our small lives,

Rampant weeds!
Rampant on meadow paths,
Rampant where vines twist around.

Year upon year
Cattle and cultivators have passed——

彼らが体内に取り込んだ放射能が
その身をこれからどのように蝕むのか
ミミズはやがて地表に這い出し
日向でのた打ち回るのだろうか
猪は背中の荒ら毛を逆立て
山じゅう狂い回るのだろうか

誰も知らない
誰も見ていない

草茫々

草茫々
田畑茫々
村一つ荒れ果てて茫々

二年前
玉蜀黍畑を風が渡り
大根の葉先に朝露が鈴生りの
その畑に
ささやかな豊かさに満ちた
その山畑に

草茫々
野道茫々
蔦かずら絡み合って茫々

幾歳月
牛を牽き　耕運機往き来し

Thousands, tens of thousands of times,
On the roads,
On the footpaths between paddies
Where people wiped away their sweat.

Rampant weeds!
Weeds surrounding our house
Burying the eaves.

In the garden where the voices of
Our children and grandchildren used to resound——
Barbeque on the fire, joyful chatter——
In the garden, where we used to have a good time
And memories of the lives we have lived never fade,

Rampant weeds!
My homeland is disappearing——
My tears flow endlessly.

Rampant weeds!
Rampant disappearing!
Rampant bitter tears!

I Took It for Granted

I took it for granted,
My life, my everyday,

何千回何万回の足跡を印した
　　　　　　　その道に
　　暮らしの汗したたり　地にしみた
　　　　　　　その畦道に

　　　　　　　草茫々
　　　　　　我が家茫々
　　　軒先を埋め尽くして茫々

　　　　　　　かつての昔
　　　子たち孫たちの歓声はね返り
　　バーベキューの焚き火燃え盛った
　　　　　　　その庭に
　　生きて暮らした思い出消えやらぬ
　　　　　　　その庭先に

　　　　　　　草茫々
　　　　　　ふるさと亡々
　　　　　　わが涙滂々

　　　　　　　草茫々
　　　　　　何もかも亡々
　　　　　　悔し涙滂々

当たり前の

　　　当たり前の暮らしが
　　当たり前であった毎日が

That this life would continue as always.
All of a sudden, a single accident——
How easily my world would collapse!

On the eastern and southern slopes
Of the mountain behind my house,
I could pick *shishitake* and *shimeji* mushrooms.
Every spring, wild angelica trees
Bear rich young shoots in the meadow west of my garden.
In the corner of my garden,
Persimmon trees bear bountiful fruit.
Under the trees, countless Japanese ginger flowers bud.
I took it for granted that I would live my ordinary life
Surrounded by nature in the Abukuma Highlands

Now I can't go into the mountains, fields and plains
Because rampant pampas grasses, mugworts
And vines forbid my entry.
It was only last year that I could walk freely in my homeland.
Now I am denied entry to my own land by rampant weeds.

I took it for granted, not realizing
How comfortable and precious it was,
My ordinary life!
I wonder if I could only have realized this
After losing what I loved, what I took for granted.

　　　　　当たり前の暮らしが
　　　　当たり前に続くと信じた日々が
　　　たった一度の事故でこんなにも脆く
　　　　崩れ去ってしまうものであろうか

　　　　すぐ裏山の東斜面や南斜面で
　　　　しし茸やサクラシメジが採れた
　　庭続きの西側の原に自生するタラの木は
　　　　　春毎に肥えた芽を吹き出した
　　　畑の片隅では茂り放題の柿が実り
　　　その根方一面に茗荷の花茎が林立し
　　　　　当たり前の自然に囲まれた
　　　阿武隈の暮らしが当たり前だった

　　　今その山や畑や草原に入ろうとしても
　　　隙間なく生い茂る芒や蓬にさえぎられ
　　　縦横にはびこるつる草に押し返され
　　　　　　行く手を阻まれるのだ
　　　　去年まで大手を振って往き来した
　　　　かけがえのないわがふるさとの
　　　　誰のものでもないわが土地への
　　　　立ち入りを草藪に拒否されるのだ

　　　　　　当たり前の暮らしが
　　　　　当たり前であった安らぎは
　　　　　　当たり前の暮らしが
　　　　　当たり前であった愛おしさは
　　　　　　失くしてしまった後でしか
　　　　気付けないものなのであろうか

Silent Village

In the village, along a slightly curved bend,
On both sides of the main street,
There are deserted houses——
No sign of life,
Not a car engine running——
Silent village.

A year and four months ago,
People bustled, engines hummed,
Dogs barked, cows mooed,
Children shouted, adults laughed.
Sounds of people living in a village
Were here.

A year and four months ago,
There were the lives of human beings,
Each one living in his or her own way
Different from one another.
Each person's dream, hope, and plan for the future
Was here.

Since the day
We were suddenly driven away
From our precious homeland,
Since the evacuation, all sounds of people have gone——

沈黙の村

わずかな傾斜の緩いカーブ
この村のメインストリートの両側に
ひっそりと立ち並ぶ人家
人の気配も　車の往き来もない
沈黙の村

一年四か月以前
そこには人間の暮らしがあった
人声のざわめきも　車の排気音も
犬の吠える声や　牛の鳴き声も
子供らの歓声や　大人たちの笑い声も
村人が生きて暮らしたすべての物音が
そこにあった

一年四か月以前
そこには人間の営みがあった
家々の形や色が違うように
それぞれの屋根の下には
それぞれの暮らしがあった
夢が　希望が　人生設計が
そこにあった

ふるさとから突如追い立てられ
村人がことごとく避難した
あの日を境に
すべての物音が途絶えてしまった

Silent village.

Going to Sleep

1.5 µSv [3] around the entrance of my house
Where daisy fleabanes bloom.
1.7 µSv under the trees
Covered with overgrown vines in my garden.
2.45 µSv on the surface of the ground
In my backyard where wet leaves pile up.

0.6 µSv around the heated table sunken into the floor
Which is no longer in use
Except during our short visits.
0.9 µSv in the sunroom
Looking out through the pane of glass.
0.8 µSv in the second floor bedroom
Where nobody has slept since the accident.

We cleaned our house after an absence of a year and four months.
Wiping away the rat droppings on the *tatami* mats
And clearing all the dust in our house that day,

---

3 The sievert (symbol: Sv) is a derived unit of ionizing radiation dose in the International System of Units (SI). It is a measure of the health effect of low levels of ionizing radiation on the human body.
One sievert equals 100 rem. The rem is an older, non-SI unit of measurement.
1 µSv is a millionth of 1 Sv and a thousandth of 1 milli Sv.

沈黙の村

寝　る

ヒメジョオンがこぞって背伸びする
玄関先で1.5μSv*
＊マイクロシーベルト
伸び放題のつる草に覆われた庭木の
根元で1.7μSv
濡れた落ち葉が堆積する裏庭の
地表で2.45μSv

一時帰宅以外使わない掘り炬燵の
周りで0.6μSv
ガラス一枚で外気と隔てられた
サンルームで0.9μSv
事故以来誰も寝ていない二階の
寝室で0.8μSv

畳の上に敷きつめたように散乱する
ネズミの糞を掃き集めた
一年四か月積りつもった家中の
埃を叩いて掃除機をかけた

We didn't manage to return
To our 0.05 µSv temporary house in Tokyo.

Near the sunken heated table
We placed floor cushions, each 0.7 µSv
And took blankets of 0.6 µSv out of the closet,
Which is now difficult to open and close.
We slept somewhere between 0.6 µSv and 0.7 µSv.

We slept shuddering in fear
Of being exposed to the radiation all night.
We slept with the knowledge
That we might not live in our house and homeland again.
Worrying about our future in the dark of night,
We slept.

> *Kashi, Kashi*
> (Half Dead, Half Dead)

Kashi, kashi, kashi   Kashi, kashi, kashi
From the very darkness at midnight
I can hear a faint sound.
It reverberates across the whole room.
Kashi, kashi, kashi   Kashi, kashi, kashi
The sound has continued non-stop
for about an hour since I was woken up.

Kashi, kashi, kashi   Kashi, kashi, kashi

　　　　　0.05μSvの都営住宅に
　　　　　帰れる時間がなくなった

　　　　　　　掘り炬燵の傍に
　　　　　0.7μSvの座布団を並べ
　　　　開け閉てが渋くなった押入れから
　　　　　0.6μSvの毛布を持ち出す
　　　　0.6μSvと0.7μSvの線量に
　　　　サンドイッチされて　寝る

　　　一晩中上下から我が身を照射する
　　　放射能の不安に怯えながら　寝る
　　　もう決して住めないに相違ない
　　　　　我が家とわがふるさと
　　　暗夜のように垂れこめる行く末を
　　　　　脳裏に刻みながら　寝る
　　　　　　　　　　　　　寝る

　　　　　　　　　　仮死々々

　　　　カシカシカシ　カシカシカシ
　　　　　　真っ暗闇の闇の底から
　　　かすかな音が部屋中に響くのである
　　　　カシカシカシ　カシカシカシ
　　　　小一時間も前に目覚めた時から
　　　その音は途切れもなく続くのである

　　　　カシカシカシ　カシカシカシ

As soon as I awoke I turned on the light
And identified the origin of the sound.
Kashi, kashi, kashi   Kashi, kashi, kashi
It's a little young rat, not even as big as an egg.

I came home for a short visit after two months absence
And was enraged to see droppings all over the *tatami* mats.
I set a rat trap and it worked.
The rat scratched the edge of the cardboard with its rear claws
Because it was trapped with its belly glued to duct tape.

Rat, rat,
You are not hurt at all.
Besides, "There are no immediate effects on your health."
I don't want to help you,
Let alone pay you compensation, or give you donations.
I only listen to you struggling, not sleeping at all.

Kashi, kashi, kashi   Kashi, kashi, kashi
I must live in a temporary shack.
Somebody might really make a fool of me if I pity you
Snickering at me beyond the darkness.
Kashi, kashi, kashi   Kashi, kashi, kashi
Kashi, kashi, kashi   Kashi, kashi, kashi
Half dead, Half dead Half dead, Half dead
Half dead, Half dead Half dead, Half dead

目覚めてすぐに電燈をつけて
物音の正体を確かめたのである
　カシカシカシ　カシカシカシ
鶏卵ほどの大きさもない
幼く小さな子鼠である

二か月ぶりの一時帰宅
畳一面真黒に散乱する
おびただしい鼠の糞に腹を立て
ネズミ捕りを仕掛けたのである
横腹を粘着剤にとらえられた鼠は
わずかにはみ出した下肢の爪先で
厚紙の端を引っ掻くのである

　　　鼠よ　鼠
おまえは今のところ痛くも痒くもない
その上「ただちに健康に影響はない」
だが俺はおまえを助けようとは決して思わぬ
ましてや義捐金や賠償を支払う気もない
おまえがしきりにもがく音を
まんじりともせず聞いているのである

　カシカシカシ　カシカシカシ
仮設の小屋に閉じ込められて
身動きならないこの俺が
おまえに憐れみをかける愚かさを
薄笑いの横目でうかがっている奴が
暗闇の向こうに必ずいるのだから………
　カシカシカシ　カシカシカシ
　カシカシカシ　カシカシカシ

From My Works Three Decades Ago

三十年前の作品から

Workers for Sub-Contractors at a Nuclear Power Plant

I drink
Sitting in a microbus after work.
I drink one can of second-grade *sake*
After working all day in the radioactivity.
I drink to get rid of my fatigue.
Tomorrow, and the day after tomorrow,
I must go on working as long as I have this job.
I drink to soothe my sorrow as a worker for sub-contractors
At a nuclear power plant.
I drink.
I drink in silence.
I drink to forget my fear.
Today again the dosimeter of exposure exceeded
100 milli REM[4] in less than 20 seconds.
I drink to ease my irritation.
Invisible poison will stick to my body
And affect my internal organs and bones
Without pain, burning or itchiness.

Today again we had many visitors.
From the tour balcony they always look down upon us
As if we were ants.

---

4 Roentgen Equivalent in Man   100 milli REM = 1 milli Sv

原発下請労働者

俺は酒を飲む
仕事帰りのマイクロバスの座席にもたれ
ワンカップの二級酒を飲む
一日中　放射能の真っ只中で
働いてきた疲れを飲む
明日も明後日も
そこで仕事にありつける限り
働き続けなければならない
原発下請労働者の悲哀を飲む
俺は酒を飲む
黙りこくって酒を飲む
今日も又100ミリレムの目盛りを
20秒足らずでふっ切った線量計の
恐怖を飲む
痛くも熱くもこそばゆくもないのに
おれの身体にこびりつき
俺の内臓や骨を変形させる物質が
眼には決して見えないと言う
いらだたしさを飲む

今日も来ていた黒山のような見物人
あいつらいつも高い展望台から
俺たちをアリのように見下ろし

They nod to each other
About the security of nuclear power plants.
It's just like people watching tigers from outside a cage——
They believe the myth that the wild animals there
Never attack human beings.
Besides, they worship the dignity in the eyes of the animals
And the ferocity of their manners.
But it is my body that knows the fear of nuclear power
Because I feel sick to my stomach,
My head aches, and my nose bleeds.

We drink.
We, workers, are picked up
By the same microbus.
On the way back from work,
We drink.
After everything, we each drink one can of second-grade *sake*.
We drink to our shared poverty.
But we have left behind somewhere
Our liveliness, our quick tempers.
We dare not step into each other's space.
We drink in silence.
One worker worries about school expenses for his son,
Another, payment for the farm equipment,
Or gift money for his brother's new house,
Or for his cousin's hospital expenses.
With all these pressing worries deep in our minds,
We sip *sake* hanging our heads low

　　　　原発の安全性についてうなずき合っている
　　　　　檻の外からこわごわ虎を覗きこみ
　　　　　　人間を襲わない猛獣の神話を
　　　　　　　　　　信じ込む
　　　　あろうことかその目付きの威厳と
　　　　　　身のこなしの獰猛さを
　　　　　　　　賛美さえもする
　　　　　だが　原発の恐ろしさは
　　　吐き気と頭痛と止まらない鼻血の
　　　　俺の身体が一番よく知っている

　　　　　　　　俺たちは酒を飲む
　　　　同じマイクロバスでかり集められた
　　　　　下請人夫は下請人夫同士
　　　　　　　仕事帰りの一杯が
　　結局二級のワンカップに落ち着いてしまう
　　　　同じ懐ろ具合の気安さを飲む
　　　　　だがかつての陽気さや
　　　喧嘩っ早さはどこかに置き忘れ
　　　　他人の座席には決して踏み込まず
　　　　　　只　黙々と酒を飲む
　　　　　息子の学費や農機具の支払い
　　　　弟の新築祝や従姉の入院など
　　　差し迫ったあれこれは腹の底に押し込め
　　　　　うつむき加減に酒をすする

Nobody claps hands and nobody answers back.
We sip *sake*.

Outside the microbus, it is raining.
It is raining and raining
On the pavement of the town at twilight.
We drive by community centers, the town hall,
The domineering gymnasium and the Center for Atomic Power.
How this town has changed
Since the nuclear power plant was constructed!
To construct the nuclear power plant,
They leveled the mountain, filled up rice fields, and
Cleared the pine tree forests.
What benefits has the nuclear power plant brought?
These ten years, my house was only renovated
With new materials for outer walls and
I added the aluminum sliding doors to the hallway.
I bought more azalea *bonsai* for my garden,
Which looks largely the same as before.

I drink.
I drink hot *sake* because I am totally exhausted.
I drink because I'm annoyed at being driven to the basement cellar,
Where we must wear big shoes and protective clothing.
I am afraid my body will be overwhelmed by radioactivity
And my flesh and bones will fester.
I drink, worrying about my life
And the future of my wife and children.

　　　　　　手拍子も二遍返しも出てこない
　　　　　　　　　　　酒をすする

　　　　　　　マイクロバスの外は雨
　　　　　暮れかけた街路のアスファルトに
　　　　　　　　　しきりと雨
　　　　　車窓を流れる公民館や役場庁舎
　　　あたりを威圧する体育館や原子力センター
　　　原発が来てから何とこの街は変わったことか
　　　　　　山を掘り崩し　田圃を埋め
　　　　松林を切り払って　我が物顔に立ち並ぶ
　　　　　　　　　原発のメリット
　　　　　　　それにしても俺の家は
　　　　　　　　　この一〇年間
　　　　　　　荒壁を新建材でふさぎ
　　　　　　廊下にサッシの戸を入れただけ
　　　　　　　変わり映えのしない庭先に
　　　　　売れるアテもない皐月の盆栽だけが
　　　　　　　　　やたらと増えた

　　　　　　　　　俺は酒を飲む
　　　　　腹の底に溜まった疲れのよどみに
　　　　　　ジンとしみ通る熱さを流し込む
　　　　　　バカでかい靴と防護服に身を包み
　　　　　　地下の穴倉に追い込まれる毎日の
　　　　　　　　　うっとうしさを飲む
　　　　　　俺の全身に放射能が充満し
　　　　　肉や骨を腐らせてゆく予感を飲む
　　　　　　　俺は俺の一生を
　　　　　　妻や子供たちの将来まで

All of us lumped together.
Then I sleep as if I were sheep
Narrowly brought back from slaughter. (*)
I sleep on the seat of the microbus,
My aching backbones scrunched in.

>Composed in 1980,
>"The Annual of the Japan Congress against
>Atomic Bombs and Hydrogen Bombs,"
>Jyugatsu-sha Publishing Company

Note on the term "slaughter"

This work was written and published 38 years ago. Back then, the word "slaughter" was widely used in daily life in Japan. However, the word has since been deemed discriminatory against workers in the meat processing industry. In Japanese, "slaughter" is now disused in public.

　　　　一緒くたに丸めこんで
　　　　苦々しげに飲みおろす
　　　　　　　それから
　　　　　　それから俺は
　　　マイクロバスの座席に
　　　痛む背中を押しつけ
かろうじて屠殺場（*）から連れ戻された
　　　　　　羊のように
　　　　　　眠りこける

　　　　（一九八〇年作・十月社刊「80原水禁」所載）

（*）本作品は今から38年前に書かれて発表されたものです。当時この言葉は日常語として一般的に使用されていました。しかしこの用語はその職場で働く人々に対して差別となる恐れがあるため、現在では「と場」と呼ばれていることを付記します。（著者註）

Adding to the Ant Tower

Morning—
On a tall bridge over the Joban Railway Line and
On the road cutting straight down to the sea
There is an endless procession of cars.
A silver grayish automobile,
Chocolate colored small microbus,
White station wagon stained with mud——
All kinds of cars in the procession from north,
South and west are gathering to the 3rd and 4th nuclear reactors
In the 2nd Nuclear Power Plant of Tokyo Electric Power Company.

The procession continues on and on along the 6th National Highway,
Stops at the traffic lights on the crossroads and
Clogs the prefectural road between Tomioka and Haramachi.
On the newly built road lined with trees,
On the street corner
Where a dog's carcass lies with its innards spilled out,
On the farmers' roads covered with half-transparent frozen snow and
On the old national road hung over by a big camellia tree,
The procession of cars goes on and on.

The humongous force
Behind the construction of the nuclear power plants
Is wads and piles of cash.

蟻たちの塔に寄せて

朝――
高い陸橋が常磐線をまたぎ
真直ぐに海へ向かう切通しの道路を
延々と続く車の列
シルバーグレーの乗用車
チョコレート色の小型マイクロバス
泥はねまみれの白いライトバン
ありとあらゆる車種の車の列が
北から　南から　西から
東京電力福島第二原子力発電所
三〜四号炉建設現場に
集ってくる

国道六号線を流れ
十字路の信号で堰きとめられ
県道富岡・原町線で渋滞し
区画整理されたばかりの街路樹の道を
臓腑のはみ出した犬の死骸の転がる街角を
残雪が半透明に凍りつく農免道路を
椿の大樹が覆いかぶさる旧国道を
どこまでも続いている

札束を煉り固め
札束を積み重ねるように
原発を建設し続ける
途方もなく巨大な力

How the procession of cars which gathers around the money
Looks exactly like the procession of ants!
Why do people build the nuclear reactor tower so high?
It's like a god who will impose a death sentence upon them.
Over the huge red and white exhaust tailpipe,
We can see the sea glittering grotesquely this morning.
The sea will be dead someday.

Once the men used to commute
To the nuclear power construction site
Secretly, not to be found by their neighbors.
As their numbers increased, one by one,
They became bold and would commute in phalanxes of cars
Yet the slight fear never goes away——
It sinks into their gut quivering like jellied fish broth.

Night——
It's dark in the fields, in the wind-barrier forest and
Around the houses in towns.
You can see the starry sky there just like before.
Yet a tragedy seems to be creeping secretly and slowly.
I wonder if the stars twinkling softly
Can peer into the town and see the tragedy.
Shapeless, colorless and odorless particles
Are constantly layering the ground.
They will accumulate in the gaps of tiled roofs and in the drainpipes,

　　　　慕い寄り群がり集まる車の流れの
　　　　何と蟻の行列に似ていることか
　　　　人は自らに死の刑罰を課す神に向かって
　　　　　　　　何故あんなにも高く
　　　　　　　塔をそそり立たせるのだろうか
　　赤白だんだらのバカでかい排気筒の向こうに
　　　　　　いつか必ず死ぬであろう海が
　　　　　　　　　　今朝もてらてらと
　　　　　　　異様に光り輝いている

　　　　　　　かつては隣近所の目を避け
　　　　　隠れるように原発に通った男たち
　　　　仲間が一人増え　二人ふえるたびに
　　　　　　　　　堂々と車を連ね
　　　　　隊伍を組んで出かけるようになった
　　　　しかし決して消えないかすかな恐怖は
　　　　　　　人々の胸の底に重く沈殿し
　　　　　　煮こごりのようにふるえている

　　　　　　　　　　　　　　夜——
　　　暗く沈む街並みや田畑や防風林の上に
　　　昔と変わらぬ澄んだ星空が広がり
　　　その下でひそかに　そしてゆっくりと
　　　　　　　　惨劇は進行する
　　　　　優しげに瞬きながらさし覗く
　　　　　　星たちには見えるだろうか
　　形もなく色も匂いもない微細な物質が
　　　　　間断なく地表に降り積もり
　　　家々の屋根瓦の隙き間や雨樋の底に

On the tips of *shungiku* greens and in the roots of winter leeks,
Inside the bones of babies and in their mothers' hair.

Inside homes
It's cozy, warm, steam rising from dishes on the table,
Children are laughing at the "Drifters," a group of comedians,
Who are moving back and forth on the TV screen.
They don't realize they are being driven into a dead end,
Oblivious to the ominousness of daily life.
Sometimes they quarrel about
The cost of hospitalization for their relatives
Sometimes they argue about
Their children's academic future.
Sometimes they have intercourse like animals.
Sometimes they pass strong-smelling gas.

The next morning——
One from Kunugidaira , two from Mujinakkubo
Men step out on cracking snow.
They exchange greetings at daybreak.
Some ride on autos with dented sides.
Others are picked up by microbuses, their paint peeling off.
They leave.
When they cross the pass in the morning glow,
In towns along the route,
From public housing with a rotten red roof

春菊の葉先や冬葱の白根に
　　赤ん坊の背骨や母親の頭髪に
　　　　　蓄積するのを………

　　　それにしても今この家で
　冬の夜の食卓に立ちのぼる湯気は
　　　　　やっぱりあたたかい
　　　テレビの画面を右往左往する
　　ドリフターズを追う子供たちの眼は
　　　　　屈託もなく笑っている
　　　　　　　　追いつめられ
　　　尚追いつめられたことを知らぬ
　　　　　　　　　強靭な日常
　　ある時は親類の病気見舞いの金額でもめ
　　ある時は子供の進学で夫婦喧嘩し
　　又ある時はけもののように睦み
　　　　　したたかな屁を放って
　　　　　　　　　　　　生きる

　　　　　　　　　　翌朝――
　むじなっ窪から二人　櫟平から一人
　キシキシと雪を踏んで男たちが出てくる
　　　暁の暗がりで声を掛けあい
　　横腹のへこんだ乗用車に乗り込み
　塗料の剥げたマイクロバスに吸い込まれ
　　　　　　　　　　出発する
　　　彼らが朝焼けの峠を越える頃
　　　　　　　　沿線の街々では
　　赤錆びたトタン屋根の町営住宅から

From the farmer's big house with the beautiful tiled roof
From the 6-tatami mat 2-room apartments
Men come out and are picked up by cars one by one,
On street corners in the bitter, freezing wind.

This morning
Countless cars make an endless procession,
Today the ant towers are sure to rise up.
Nuclear power reactors will grow
Grotesquely day after day
Like an ominous prediction.

   Composed in 1981, Ibid.

瀬戸瓦の堂々たる構えの農家の玄関から
六畳二間のアパートの階段から
吐き出された男たちが
凍てつく風の街角で
次々と車にひろわれる

こうして今朝も
無数の車が延々と列を作り
こうして今日も
蟻たちの塔が確実に積み上げられ
原発は不吉な予言のように
日々その醜悪な姿をあらわにしてくる

（１９８１年作・前掲書）

An Epitaph

Nemoto Sadao, 59 years old,
lived in Okuma-cho, Futaba County, Fukushima Prefecture.
Early morning on February 26th, 1979,
He died in Kyoritsu Hospital in Iwaki city.
The cause of his death was "celebral meningitis."

In November 1946, he returned from war
And settled in a clearing deep in the forest,
About 6.5 km away from his parents' house.
The next year he married a distantly-related girl
And they lived there together.
For years they cultivated their paddies and fields, kept livestock.
They gradually increased their crop year by year, little by little.
Soon two children arrived: a boy and a girl.
However, the time came
That he could not manage to live solely on agriculture.
So for years he had to go and work in Tokyo during the winter.

In June 1961,
Right after rice seedlings were planted in the paddies,
He was hired by a local construction company, Takeuchi Komuten.
He made frames to be used in concrete ditches for roads.
Three months later he moved to another company,
Sakanaka Kogyo in Tomioka city.

聞き書きの墓碑銘

根本定男　五九歳
福島県双葉郡大熊町在住
54年2月26日未明
いわき市　協立病院で死亡
病名「脳髄膜炎」

21年11月　外地から復員した男は
実家から6.5キロ山奥の開拓地に
山林を切り払って単身入植し
翌年　遠縁の娘をめとって住みついた
数年かけて田畑を拓き　家畜を飼った
作物はわずかながら年々収穫を増し
やがて男女二人の子をもうけた
だが追い打ちをかけるように
百姓だけでは食えない時代がきた
出稼ぎの長い年月が続いた

46年6月　田植えが一段落した直後から
地元の土建業・竹谷工務店に雇われ
取り付け道路側溝の
コンクリ仮ワク作りをやった
三ヶ月程で富岡町の坂中工業に移り

Since then he worked and changed sub-construction companies
One after the other.
One company didn't pay well enough for the work he did.
Another fired him.
Others went bankrupt.
Depending on where he was employed, his work differed.
Depending on what his work entailed, his pay went up or down.
Despite the lack of security in being a day laborer,
He had a job as long as
He milled around the nuclear power plant like a worker ant.

When he wasn't paid enough for construction work,
He shifted to regular check-ups for nuclear power reactors.
He often went to
The limted access areas of nuclear power plants;
Sometimes he wore B clothes, and other times C clothes.
ID pass number 174866 Nemoto Sadao.
He did all kinds of work, except cleaning the reactors.
He could not remember the names of every work section
Because the reactor is too huge and too complicated.
In March 1977 he was hired by a company, Yamawaki Koji.
He cleaned the house boiler regularly in a nuclear power plant.
In the reactor, the air was thick with dust,
He sanded down the boiler and painted it with colored paint.
In C clothes it was so hot and humid that he sweated and sweated.
He got so fed up that
He tore off his protective mask and
Flung it to the ground because it was stifling.

以降原発建設の下請け・孫請けを
転々と渡り歩いた
転職のきっかけは賃金不払いだったり
解雇だったり　倒産だったりした
職場が変わるたびに　仕事が変わり
仕事が変わるたびに　賃金が上下した
不安定な日雇い稼業だったが
原発周辺を蟻のように徘徊していれば
どこかで仕事にありつけた

建設の仕事が先細ると定険に回り
管理区域にも絶えず出入りした
Ｂ服の時も　Ｃ服の時もあった
従事者パスＮＯ１７４８６６号
根本定男
ランドリー以外の仕事はほとんどやった
だが原発の構造はばかでかく複雑で
作業箇所の名称すら満足に覚えられなかった
52年３月から　山脇工事に雇われた
定険毎にハウスボイラーの掃除をやった
空中に濃い粉塵が充満する原子炉で
サンダーをかけ　カラーチックを塗った
Ｃ服は蒸し暑く全身を脂汗が伝い
無性にイライラした
息苦しい防護マスクに腹を立て
むしり取って床に叩きつけると

His throat got sore because of the minute iron powder,
Floating in the air, sticking to the surface of his throat.
His manager ran over and rubbed his head in warning.
That day, all morning, he felt nauseous and
Had a headache in the back of his head.
His pocket dosimeter showed
110 milli REM of radiation, which was recorded
In haste on his pass card to the nuclear reactor.

Since then he started to cough a lot.
Sometimes he would spit out black phlegm.
The following September, Yamawaki Koji Company went bankrupt.
The president disappeared.
The health check records which he had undergone quarterly
Were sent from one company to another.
The radiation exposure card he himself was never allowed to see also
Disappeared——
For four months after the bankruptcy
He did nothing, killing time at home.
He coughed and coughed and felt utterly listless.
The phlegm which he spit from his bed
Stuck to the window and covered it in black dots.
One night he felt the need to urinate but could not.
He went to the toilet every five minutes.
The next morning
He went to see doctors at Futaba Prefectural Hospital.
Without being told the name of the disease,
He was sent to Okuma Mental Hospital.

浮遊する微細な鉄粉が喉に突き刺さり
駆けつけた放管に頭をこずかれた
その日　午前中吐き気止まらず
後頭部が痛んだ
ポケット線量計は
110ミリレムを示し
入域カードに乱暴な数字で記録された

この頃から次第に咳がひどくなり
真黒な痰がでた
翌年９月　山脇工事は倒産し
社長が失踪した
そして三ヶ月毎の定期検診の記録も
会社から会社ヘタライ廻しされ
本人がついぞ目にすることのなかった
被爆手帳も
同時にこの世から消えてしまった
倒産後四ヶ月　家でブラブラした
咳はますますひどく異常にけだるかった
寝たままふっ切った痰は
サッシの窓に吐きつけられ
黒く点々とこびりついた
ある夜　尿意はあっても放尿できず
夜通し五分置きに便所に立った
翌朝　県立双葉病院で診察を受けた
病名も告げられぬまま大熊精神病院に移され

He was to be hospitalized for alcoholism,
Though he could only down one small bottle of *sake* at most.
Three days later, his family were notified
That he was in critical condition.
They went to the hospital and saw him
Constantly vomiting something
Like chocolate from his swollen belly.
He was taken immediately
To Kyoritsu Hospital in Iwaki city by ambulance.
He was diagnosed with "celebral meningitis,"
Which was very rare except in children.

Two months later he died, and
Though his family and his friends remembered him,
His existence in the world was forgotten and erased.
Nemoto Sadao, 59 years old
We don't have any documents now
To prove a relationship between his death and radiation exposure
Over his career.
Nothing at all.

    Composed in 1982, Ibid.

　　　　　　銚子一本が関の山だった男が
　　　　　アルコール中毒症で入院させられた
　　三日後　危篤の知らせで駆けつけた家族は
　　　　　　　腹部が異様にふくれ上がり
　　　　　口からチョコレート色の吐瀉物を
　　　　　絶え間なく流し続ける男と対面した
　　　　　　　　即座に救急車で
　　　　いわき市　協立病院に運ばれた男は
　　　通常小児以外ほとんどかかることのない
　　　　　　「脳髄膜炎」と診断された

　　　　　　　　　　二ヶ月後
　　　　　　　　　男は死亡した
　　　家族や知人たちのおぼろげな記憶の他には
　　　　　　　生きてきた痕跡のすべてを
　　　　　　　　抹消されてしまった男
　　　　　　　　根本定男　五九歳
　　　今　この男の職歴と放射能被曝を証明し
　　　死に至る疾病との因果関係を証拠だてる
　　　　　　　　　一切の資料はない

　　　　　　　　　　　　　註：年号は昭和

　　　　　　　　　　（一九八二年作・前掲書）

Autumn Castle Fortress

Is it not a castle fortress,
Erected on the march to modernity?
The concrete wall is like a cliff
Closely resembling the stone wall foundations
Of a warrior's castle.
Peasants were once conscripted
To roll stone slabs on logs
And haul soil and gravel in rope baskets.
Now their descendents are busy
Squandering concrete, pouring it into high frames
At the construction sites of nuclear power plants——
Nothing but an eternal waste.

The high stone walls were
For hiding bloody internal conflicts in the castle
Rather than for protecting against intruders.
Once plots, revenges, bloodshed, and executions
Were hidden from the common folk.
Now nobody can see the countless cracks and pinholes
In the heat exchangers, pressure vessels and fuel rods.
Nobody can see the radioactivity
Filling the nuclear reactor buildings.

秋の城

もはやそれは
現代を踏み従えてたちはだかる
城砦ではなかったか
断崖のようにそそり立つ
コンクリートの隔壁は
戦国時代の巨大な石積みに
なんと似ていることか
コロをかって切り石を動かし
モッコで土砂をかついだ
かつての民百姓が
今　原発建設現場で
コンクリ仮枠を高々と組み
果てしない浪費のように生コンを送りこむ
作業に追われている

四囲を圧する石垣の高さは
外敵の侵入を拒むよりも
城砦の内部で絶えず噴き出す
膿みや血糊を外へ漏らさないための
防壁であったろうか
その昔　城内で繰り広げられた
陰謀や報復　刃傷や誅殺が
決して民衆の眼に
さらされることのなかったように
熱交換器や圧力容器や燃料棒に
うがたれた無数の亀裂やピンホール
原子炉建屋に充満する放射性物質を
その目で見た者はいない

The nuclear power plants need countless men
Who must work, regardless of radiation exposure limit,
On repairs in case of trouble,
Or for periodical checks-ups of the reactors.
Unresistingly scrapped workers
Were sent to hospital after hospital in the vicinity.
They died one after another.
Workers who constructed the castle fortress
Were killed because they knew too many secrets
About the castle's inner workings.
Across the ages,
Voiceless victims are sent to underground prisons.
Right under the nuclear reactors,
Inside the basement storage tank,
Is the waste liquid of enriched uranium.
The tank is full of it.
It is a curse, bound to the history of the castle.

Whether it's from pine forests or paddies of ripe rice kernels
Or from the roof-tops of the town halls,
As far as the red and white exhaust pipes can be seen,
These towns and villages are completely dominated
By the big money of the electric company.
Once the *samurai* lord of the Warring States period
Could see his territory, thousands of hectares of rice paddies
From the lattice window on the top of his castle.
He built his castle at the hub of transportation
Gripping the heart of the economy in his fist.

故障修理や定期点検作業に投入され
被曝の限度を超えて使役される人間は
　　　　　　　　　　数知れない
無抵抗にスクラップされた労働者は
　　　　付近の病院をタライ廻しされ
　　　　　　　次々と死んでいった
かつて築城の機密に通じた土工たちが
　　　　　　人知れず消されたように
　　　　　　　物言わぬ人柱には
　　　いつの世にも周到に用意された
　　　　　　　　　　地下牢がある
　　　　　　　　　　　原発の真下
　　　　　　　　地底の貯蔵タンクには
　　　　　　濃縮廃液がたたえられ
城館の来歴にまつわる呪いのように
どんよりと静まりかえっている

　　　　　　　それが松林の上であれ
　　　穂を垂れた稲田の向こうであれ
あるいは役場庁舎の屋上からであれ
赤白だんだらの排気筒が見える限りの
　　　　　　　　　　町々や村々は
　　　巨大な電力資本の支配の枠組みに
　　　　　　　すっぽりと囲い込まれた
　　　　　　　　交通の要衝に城を構え
　　　経済の中枢を握って君臨した
　　　　　　　　　　戦国の武将たち
そびえたつ天守閣の格子窓からは
　　　　　　　　何萬石もの領地が
　　　　　　　一望に見渡せたであろう

However, over the course of history
The white walls of the castle were destroyed
And its foundation weathered.
The castle fortress which was once impenetrable
Is now frequented by many tourists.
They stop casually at the ruins of an ancient age.
The mossy stone walls with red ivy growing in autumn——

Will the day come
When those enormous nuclear reactor buildings collapse
And become a heap of ruins,
With moss creeping over?

Autumn——
Tokyo Electric Power Company's Fukushima Nuclear Power Plants-
They stand strong in a line
On the coast of the Pacific Ocean,
Where whitecaps lap the shore.
They are not only plants for power generation
Polluted with radioactivity.
Dominating people and staying at the heart of the economy,
They are modern castle fortresses.
Under the crisp autumn sunlight,
Colossal white turbine buildings stand aloft.
Inside the turbines
A contradiction of this age is
Revolving with a roar.

      Composed in 1983, Ibid.

だが歴史の変遷は
城門の白壁を崩し土台石を風化させる
かつて難攻不落を誇った城砦は
　今　訪れた観光客が
気まぐれに足をとどめる
旧時代の遺跡でしかない
苔むした石垣に
真っ赤に紅葉した蔦を這わせて………

いつの時にか
この巨大な原子炉建屋が
累々と崩れ落ち
苔むす日があろうか

秋──
太平洋の白波が打ち寄せる海岸線に
整然と立ち並ぶ
東京電力福島原子力発電所
もはやそれは
単に放射性物質にまみれた
発電施設と言うにとどまらない
民衆を支配し
経済の中枢に腰をすえた
現代の城砦に他ならぬ
透明な秋の陽差しを浴びて立ち尽くす
白亜の巨大なタービン建屋
その中で唸りをあげて
回転するものは
時代の矛盾である

（一九八三年作・前掲書）

Nuclear Power Plant: A Dialogue

Wanna hear about nuclear power plants?
OK, I'll tell you.
Oh! You're treating today?
Shochu highball?
I prefer the stuff straight.
How are things?
If everything were OK, would I be drinking
At a shabby bar like this?
You know, we aren't paid by the hour
We're paid according to our exposure to radioactivity.
Who cares how the economy is in the world?

I first came to this town 15 years ago.
I started to work for a sub-contractor of K Construction Company.
My first job was to construct the turbine structures.
We called it 'building the swallow's nest."
In order to build turbine walls,
We poured in fresh concrete using a hydraulic pump.
A lot of gaps appeared in the corners and
Behind the steel framing of the wall.
We had to stuff more fresh concrete in by hand.
It was difficult to get my hands in
Because the steel frames were too complicated.
I did a real sloppy job, shoving the damned stuff

原発問答

原発の話が聞きてえ？
それぁ話ぐれぇしたって悪かねぇが………
え？　おごってくれんの？
チューハイ？　なぁにハイ抜きで結構
景気？　誰が景気よくってこんな
赤提灯にハイヒール履かせたみてぇな
「すなっく」で酒飲んでるかよ
大体俺たちは時間なんぼの日当と違って
線量当たりなんぼの賃金だ
世間並の景気なんざ通用しねぇのよ

俺が初めてこの町にきたのぁ一五年前だ
K建設の下請けで稼ぐことになって
手始めの仕事が「燕の巣作り」よ
タービン建屋の隔壁作んのに
油圧ポンプ車で生コンぶっこむんだが
鉄骨の陰とか角にやたらと隙間ができる
そのジャンカに後から生コンで
ダンゴ作って手で詰め込む訳よ
鉄骨組み合わさってて満足に腕がはいらねぇ
そん時は手前の方だけふさいで
うわっつら壁塗りして置くだけだ

Into the turbine walls.

It was like an old Japanese radish ridden with holes.

Soon the construction work was almost finished.
My boss took me to the inspections department
For the nuclear reactors.
When I first peered into the reactor,
I was astonished.
The inside was a dark cobalt blue——
There is no such color in the world——
Water so pure and blue that
Whoever saw it would be entranced.
If I fell in, all my flesh and bones might melt away.

After that?
I went to Tsuruga and Hamaoka.5
Accidents?
What was I worried about?
One guy was transported to a hospital by helicopter, never to return.
Another pissed and pooped all over the place and died.
Another guy committed suicide at dawn
Hanging himself from the beam of a prefab home.
He had complained all night about an unbearable headache.
What about me?
Hmmm… It was early in the morning
At the beginning of spring two years ago,

---

5 Both are the names of the cities where nuclear power plants were constructed.

隔壁なんつったっておめえ
つまりはスの入った大根よ

その内建設の仕事が先細りになって
親方の世話で定検に廻ったんだが
初めてリアクターに入って
釜ん中覗きこんだ時にゃあ
まったくビックラこいたもんなぁ
コバルトブルーのもっと濃いやつで
この世にあんな色は他にねぇ
落ちたら肉も骨もグダグダに
とろけっちまうに違いねぇ
なんだか身体ごと引きずりこまれそうな
真っ青な水の色よ

それから？
あぁ　敦賀にも行ったし浜岡にも行った
事故？　心配はかどんなって………
それぁおめえ　ヘリで運ばれてって
それっきり帰ってこねぇ奴もいれば
大小便垂れ流しで死んだ奴もいる
「頭割れそうだ」なんて一晩中くどいてて
明け方飯場の梁から
ワイヤーでぶら下がってた奴もいたさ
てめえのことを言えって？
んー　あれぁおととしの春先だったな

There was an accident in the storage tank
With concentrated uranium waste,
So I went down to the basement.
A pipe was broken,
and the floor was flooded with water.
I had to change pipes, getting soaked in the waste water.
My radioactive alarm was malfunctioning.
I had almost 150 REM.
When I got back outside, I had a headache and felt nauseous.
I rested in the office for the rest of the day.
The next day I've got eczema all over my body.
The company doctor gave me a shot
And prescribed some medicines.
He hardly listened to me about the accident.
I went to see one doctor after another
In various hospitals and clinics in the neighboring towns.
Every doctor says, "It's just eczema."
When rumors spread that I went to see doctors,
People at the office watched me warily and
Even my bubbly landlady treated me with indifference.
"They're all in cahoots with each other," I thought.
I quit the three-month job after half a month out of fear.

Why did I go back to this work?
I have been a seasonal worker for about 15 years.
I am treated like royalty at home for a week or so

朝っぱら濃縮廃液貯蔵タンクで
事故だってんで地下に降りた
配管ぶっ裂けて床は水浸しよ
頭から廃液かぶってパイプ交換だ
アラームはパンクするし
150近くも線量食った
表に出たら頭痛はするし吐き気はするで
いちんち事務所でゴロゴロしてたんだが
翌る日んなったら身体中ブツブツの湿疹だ
指定医は注射打って薬出すだけで
事故の話なんざてんで聞き流しよ
隣町にも行って病院や町医者を
片っ端から当たってみたが奴ら口をそろえて
「只の発疹です」
俺が医者巡りしてるって噂がたつと
事務所の連中の目付きが変わってきた
下宿のおかみさんもよそよそしくなった
「こいつらぁみんなグルだ」
そう思ったらにわかにおっかなくなって
三ヶ月契約を半月でケツ割って
逃げ帰ったものよ

そいつがなんで又舞い戻った？
俺ぁ一五年この方出稼ぎやってんだ
盆正月に一週間10日帰る分には
チヤホヤお客さん扱いだが

When I come back for the Bon Festival[6] or for New Year's.
But when I spend six months or a year idling at home,
My family kicks me out of my own home.
Sooner or later I get the message.
Children? Four of them finished school and are working.
My eldest son married and they are expecting a baby.
Me, a gypsy? The title feels too fancy for me.
I'm a true vagabond of nuclear power plants.
Hey, I've probably already been sucked into
The cobalt blue water of the reactor.
I am stuck floundering in it until I die.
I think that's my destiny.
What? You don't agree?
Come on! Get real kiddo……

    Composed in 1984, Ibid.

---

6 During the Bon Festival in August, the souls of ancestors seem to return home.

半年・一年ゴロタラしてた日にゃーおめえ
この家に俺のいる席なんざどこにもねぇ
　　　そいつが段々分かってくらぁな
子供？　四人共学校終わって就職した
跡取り夫婦にゃ孫できるばっかしよ
ジプシー？　そんな気の利いたもんか
　　　正真正銘　原発無宿の流れ者よ
　　　　もしかしたら俺ぁ
リアクターの釜ん中の真っ青な水に
とうの昔に引きずりこまれていて
死ぬまでもがきまわっている
それが本当の俺の姿なのかも知れねぇなぁ
　　　　違うか？　え？
　　　　おい　若ぇの……

　　　　　　　　　　（一九八四年作・前掲書）

I Can Hear

Sometimes deep in my ears
I would hear a faint sound resonating
Far in the distance.
Was it just an auditory hallucination?
Or did I really hear it?
The sound always evokes a scene
That has left a strong impression on me.
When I was a little boy,
I used to blow into an empty bottle of beer
And make a whistling sound.
The howling sound conjures up
A vast plain of withered grass.

In winter toward the end of the war,
I evacuated from Tokyo to a village
In the mountains of Abukuma.
It was a remote place distant from towns.
All the forests of various trees, terraced fields,
And thatched roofs were covered with snow.
On a freezing starry night,
I could hear the faint whistle
Of a locomotive on the Banetsu-tosen Line 15 km away.
My grandfather used to mutter to himself,
"It's going to snow again."

聴こえる

　　　時々　耳の底で
　かすかに鳴っているような
　遠い物音を聴くことがある
　果たしてあれは幻聴だったろうか
　本当に聴こえたのであろうか
　物音は決まって脳裡に刻みつける
　ひとつの情景を伴ってひびいた
　　　たとえば幼い日
　ビール瓶の口に息を吹きこんで
　　野太い笛の音をたてた
　びょうびょうと鳴るそのひびきは
　私の内部に茫漠とした枯草の曠野を
　　　徐々に広げ始める

　　　　　終戦まぎわの冬
　阿武隈の襞々にへばりついて
　ひっそりと息づいている村落に
　　　　疎開してきた
　雑木山も段畑も茅葺き屋根も
　　すっぽりと雪に埋もれ
　星たちが空一面に凍りついている夜
　一五キロ先を走る磐越東線の汽笛が
　　かすかに聴こえることがあった
　　　　「又雪になるぞい」
　祖父のつぶやきをぼんやりと聞きながら
　　　　電車やビルや
　アドバルーンや街路樹の風景を
　かけがえのない故郷のように

I used to recall trains, buildings, advertising balloons,
And all the scenery along tree-lined streets—
Precious memories of my home.

In summer, B 29 air fighters sometimes
Flew high in the sky here.
I could only hear their roaring, but not see them.
Afterward, winds blew slowly through the grass,
On the banks of paddy fields.
Then I thought I heard the sound of waves far in the distance.
Was it just the wind blowing through cedar forests?
In the heart of the Abukuma mountains far from the ocean,
It reminded me of the hot sand of Zushi Beach
And the burning heat on my feet.

Sometimes deep in my ears I would hear a faint sound
Resonating from far in the distance.
When I was soaking in an old- fashioned bath tub
In a hut with corrugated tin roof, I would hear the sound of
Mountain streams in intonation high and low.
After the war
I continued to live in the valley of the mountains of Abukuma
Where neither buses nor electricity reached.
I used to count the cracking sounds of trees
In the woods behind my house all night.
Trees were covered with snow so heavy that
Some of them toppled over.
The sound of snow falling and accumulating—

　　　　　　　思い起こしていた
　　　　　　　　夏になって
　　　　　　　時々高空をＢ29が
　　　　　見えない爆音をひびかせては過ぎた
　　　　　　　　そしてそのあとは
　　　　　　　田圃の土手の草いきれを
　　　　　　風がゆっくりゆすって通った
　　　　　　　　　　その時
　　　　　　　　遙かに潮騒の音を
　　　　　　　　聴いたように思った
　　　　　　　あれは山蔭の杉森を渡る
　　　　　　　風のざわめきであったろうか
　　　　　　海には遠い阿武隈の山懐ろで
　　　　　　かつて遊んだ逗子の浜の
　　　　　　　　灼けた砂の熱さを
　　　　　　蹠にひりひりよみがえらせた
　　　　　　　時々　耳の底で
　　　　　　かすかに鳴っているような
　　　　　　遠い物音を聴くことがある
　　　　　　端板を打ちつけた小屋の
　　　　　古びた据え桶の風呂に浸っていると
　　　　　　　谷川の音が高く低く
　　　　　　　抑揚をつけて聴こえた
　　　　　　　　　戦後――
　　　　　バスも電気もない阿武隈の山峡に
　　　　　　　そのまま住みつき
　　　　　　裏山の樹々が雪に折れる音を
　　　　　　夜通し数えて暮らした
　　　　　　　雪の降り積む音は

Was I hearing it? Or was I not?

Forty years have passed since then,
Roads have been paved and buses are running.
Along the coastal line, which feels somehow nearer,
Nuclear power plants have been constructed,
Huge exhaust pipes in a row.
At night,
I felt that I could hear the sound of cold winter wind
Whistling at the mouth of the exhaust pipes
Like on an empty bottle of beer.
Tonight again,
The exhaust pipes must be whistling
In the pine forests 30 km away.
Radioactive substances emitted from the pipes
Pile up on the sleeping towns and villages.
They wither the land as far as the pipes can be seen
And change it to a wasteland.

Sometimes deep in my ears I can hear a sound
Resonating slightly in the distance.
I am in my room whose window frame is so tight
That I can neither hear the whistle of trains in the distance
Nor the stream flowing in the valley.
Yet I can hear the sound of radioactive substances
Falling and piling up all over the ground,
Though they are colorless, shapeless, odorless.

      Composed in 1985, Ibid.

　　　　耳に聴こえているようでもあり
　　　　聴こえていないようでもあった

　　　　　あれからすでに四十年
　　　道路が舗装され　バスが走った
　　　にわかに距離を縮めた海岸線に
　　　　　原子力発電所が建設され
　　　どでかい排気筒が立ち並んだ
　　　　　　暗夜——
　　　その排気口に木枯らしが吹きつけて
　　　　ビール瓶のように音立てるのを
　　　　　　聴いたように思った
　　　今夜も又三十キロ先の松原の中で
　　　　　びょうびょうと鳴り続ける
　　　　　　　排気筒よ
　　　その口から吐き出す放射性物質は
　　　寝静まる町々や村々に降りしきり
　　　そこから見える限りの風景を
　　　　　曠野のように枯らすのだ

　　　　　　時々　耳の底で
　　　　かすかに鳴っているような
　　　　遠い物音を聴くことがある
　　　今はもう遙かな汽笛も　谷川の音も
　　　決して聞こえないサッシの窓の部屋にいて
　　　　色も　形も　匂いもない物質が
　　　　　地表一面に降り積もる音を
　　　　　　聴くことがあった

　　　　　　　　　　（一八八五年作・前掲書）

Fires

At 6:42 am on August 31st, 1985
A fire broke out at the turbine building of the 1st nuclear reactor
In the 1st Fukushima Nuclear Power Plant of
Tokyo Electric Power Company.
The alarm which connects to the turbine started
In the central operation room.
The fire alarm screeched.
Officers on duty rushed to the turbine building.

  Just then
  Both the town halls and the county fire stations were fast asleep.
  From Tokyo Electric Power Company
  No notice was sent out.

At 7:10 am
Three officers started to extinguish the fire.
Electric receptors burned out.
There was a blackout in the turbine building and head office.
Fire spread through electric cables.
About one hour later the fire had not yet been extinguished.
The turbine building was filled with smoke
Which flowed out through cable ducts.

  Just then

火　災

1985年8月31日午前6時42分
東京電力福島第一原子力発電所
1号機タービン建屋で火災発生
中央操作室の地絡警報器が作動
火災警報器がけたたましく鳴動
当直員がただちに現場へ急行した

その時刻
町役場も
広域消防署も
朝の眠りの底に沈んでいた
東京電力からは何の連絡も
発せられなかった

午前7時10分
駆けつけた職員3名が消火活動を開始
受電盤が焼き切れ
タービン建屋と事務本館が停電
火は更に電源ケーブルを伝って燃え広がり
ほゞ一時間を経過して
尚衰えを見せなかった
煙はタービン建屋に充満し
ケーブルダクトから外へ噴き出した

その時刻

   Children were walking to school in single file
   On the foot paths between rice fields
   Connecting to farmers' roads
   Or on the pedestrian overpass at the crossing
   At National Highway 6.

At 8:07 am, they called the fire station.
At 8:10 am, they called the prefectural office.
It was about an hour and half after fire broke out.
Both fire departments at Namie and Tomioka
Sent 15 fire engines altogether.
They surrounded the 1st nuclear reactor building.
No one could go inside the radioactive control area;
They poured water into the building
Removing the duct from outside.
At 8:50 am
The fire was extinguished, two hours later after it had occurred.

   On March 15, 1980 a fire occurred—
     No one called the fire department.
   On May 21, 1981 another fire occurred—
     No one called the fire department.
   On April 2, 1982 a fire occurred at the 2nd turbine building—
     They told the fire department on May 12.
   On March 15, 1985 a fire occurred at the 5th turbine building—
     They told the fire department on April 2.
     (One person suffered severe burns.)
   Futaba County Fire Department announced

　　　　　　農免道路に通じる畦道を
　　　　　　六号国道交差点の歩道橋を
　　　　　　　登校の子供らが
　　　　　　一列に並んで歩いていた

　　　　　午前8時7分　119番通報
　　　　　午前8時10分　県庁に通報
　　　　火災発生から約1時間半後であった
　　　　　　浪江・富岡両消防署から
　　　　　　　消防車15台が出動し
　　　　　　　一号機周辺を固めたが
　　　　　放射能管理区域立ち入りが出来ず
　　　　　外部からダクトをはずして注水
　　　　　　　　午前8時50分
　　　　出火から約2時間後ようやく鎮火した

　　　　　55年3月15日　発生火災
　　　　　　　消防署通報〜なし
　　　　　56年5月21日　発生火災
　　　　　　　消防署通報〜なし
　　57年4月2日　二号機タービン建屋火災
　　　　　　消防署通報〜5月12日
　　60年3月15日　5号機タービン建屋火災
　　　消防署通報〜4月2日（重火傷1名）
　　　　双葉広域消防本部は東京電力に対し

   That they would protest against Tokyo Electric Power Company.

On September 2
Authorities from the relevant institutions
In Fukushima prefecture, Futaba and Okuma towns,
Inspected the fire accident zone.
However, they could not find the reason
For the delay in reports of the fires.
Institutionalized concealment of the accidents is to blame
For the delays in reports of the fires.
The cause of the fires is still unknown.

   So I rode my second-hand motorbike
   And went to the neighborhoods of Futaba and Okuma.
   On the farmers' roads in the sizzling hot day
   I said to people around, "We residents are treated
   As if we couldn't hear or see.
   We have no chance of notification when an accident occurs."
   I told the laughing women having a rest under trees
   From their construction work on the roads.
   I told a sullen young mechanic,
   Who got up from under the car…

"They called the fire department one and half hours after the fire.
They never disclosed the cause of the fire."
I expressed my indignation to the old guy in the tractor
Who was busy collecting dried grass in the middle of the field.
Then a guy, who seemed to be a Sunday farmer,

　　　　　厳重に申し入れを行うと表明した

　　　　　　　　　　９月２日
　　　　　県　双葉・大熊両町などの
　　　　関係機関立ち入り調査が実施された
　　　しかしあまりにも体質化した事故隠しが
　　　　通報遅延の根本要因である事実は
　　　　　　決して暴かれはしなかった
　　　　　　　しかも出火原因は
　　　　　依然として不明のままである

　　　　　　　　　そこで俺は
　　　　　　中古のバイクにまたがって
　　　カンカン照りの野良道を往ったり来たり
　　　「住民は耳も目もふさがれている
　　事故が起きたって知らされるアテなんかねぇ」
　　　　　　　と説いてまわる
　　　　　樹蔭にたむろして笑いこける
　　　　道路工事のオバちゃんたちに
　　　車の下から無愛想な仰向け顔で
　　這い出してくる修理工の若者に………

　　「火災が起きたって通報は一時間半も後だ
　　　原因だってまだ公表されちゃいない」
　　牧草畑の真ん中で乾草集めに大わらわの
　　　　　　トラクターの親父さんに
　　　　俺はしきりと憤懣をぶちまける

Grinned, sweat all over his bearded face,
And said to me,
"The cause of the fire?
Ahaha! Don't you know?
It should be the fire itself!"
Again
Nuclear power is safe
Beyond reason.

        Composed in 1986, Ibid.

すると汗まみれの髭面をニヤリと崩して
日曜百姓の親父は言ってのける
「火事の原因だぁ？
アハハ　そんなものぁおめえ
火だぁべぇ？　」
かくて又
原発は故なくも安全である

註：一部年号は昭和

（一九八六年作　前掲書）

Epilogue: War, Nuclear Power, and My Work

I was born in Setagaya, Tokyo and brought up there till I was in the third grade at Kamikitazawa Elementary School. At that time, I was weak and my doctor diagnosed that I had bronchial asthma. He advised that I should go to the countryside for fresh air. Besides, the Pacific War had intensified and US bomb raids came to Tokyo several times. I was transferred to a school in Fukushima where my mother's parents lived.

It was in the autumn of my third grade when I was sent to live with my grandparents in a village in the mountains of Fukushima. Upon my arrival, my grandfather took me to the nearby mountain to pick mushrooms. Among these many beautiful, colored mushrooms, like *sakura-shimeji*, *koganehoki-dake*, and *murasaki-shimeji*, I was strongly attracted to the *inohana* or the 'nose of the wild boar', which is brownish gray and has extraordinary lamellae. Even now I wonder why I felt such a strong attraction.

In 1945, the war ended and I stayed in Fukushima. My father was a civil servant and technological scientist in the military. That's why he was so frightened by the American occupation. In September, one month after defeat in war, my family. Settled in Katsurao village, even deeper in the mountains than my grandparents' house.

There were huge *inohana* mushrooms of diameter 20 to 25 cm growing one upon another in Katsurao. I began to wander around mountains near my house as if it were my garden and looked for mushrooms and other edible mountain plants. Katsurao village

来歴・三題
　——あとがきに代えて——

　私は東京・世田谷に生まれ育ち、小学校三年生まで「上北沢小学校」に在籍しました。当時私は体が弱く医者からは「気管支炎」（今で言う小児喘息？）と診断され転地を勧められたこともあり、又その時期太平洋戦争が激化しつつあって、東京にもアメリカの爆撃機が何度か飛来し始めた頃でもあったため、疎開の形で母親の実家である福島に転校しました。

　福島の山村に単身疎開したのは小学校三年生の秋。早速祖父に連れられて、付近の山へ茸を採りに出かけました。それにしてもサクラシメジや黄金篶茸・ムラサキシメジなど、色の美しい茸が数ある中で、地味な茶鼠色に怪異と言っていいヒダを持つイノハナ（学名・香茸）に、強く惹かれたのは何故だったろうか。今も不思議に思います。

　昭和二十年、そのまま福島で終戦を迎えました。父親は軍属で科学技術者。そのためアメリカ軍の進駐を極度に恐れ、終戦の翌九月、母方の実家からより山深い葛尾村に移住し、直径二〇〜二五センチのイノハナが折り重なって道を引く、山あいの林の中に入植しました。付近の山をわが庭のように歩き回り、茸や山菜を探しまわる日々がそこから始まり、この地が第二の故郷となりました。

became a second home to me.

Eventually I settled down in Katsurao and worked for a local post office. I got married and raised three children. They grew up to find jobs and marry in Tokyo. I have eight grandchildren who used to visit Katsurao village not only during summer or winter holidays, but also on spring or autumn breaks. They were accustomed to the way of life in the mountains. I used to send them spring mountain plants and autumn mushrooms as soon as I picked them. One of my children intended to move back to Fukushima after retirement and was looking for a place to live. My children and grandchildren were deprived of our home by the nuclear accident, not to mention us, an old couple.

"Is there a Mr. Kojima here?"

A plump man visited me in the post office where I worked. He shouted out for me in so loud a voice that everyone in the whole office could hear. He was Mr. Iwamoto Tadao, who was a member of the Futaba Town Assembly. I was in my mid-twenties and worked as a clerk at the small post office in the countryside. Mr. Iwamoto, who was dark skinned and had big eyes, asked me passionately to join his activities. "I'd like you to help me set up the Association for Protecting the Constitution throughout Futaba County. It should be, in actuality, an organization to support the anti-nuclear power movement." Then we started to prepare. Mr. Iwamoto became chairman and I, chief secretary. This organization was a pioneer of the anti-nuclear power movement in Futaba County. Though it focused on fighting against nuclear power, it had to be camouflaged by another name. This was because there were complicated local problems in Futaba County.

そのまま葛尾村に定住し、地元の郵便局に就職。結婚して三人の子供を育て、成人した子供たちは全員東京で就職・結婚し、八人の孫たちは夏・冬休みは勿論、ゴールデンウィークや秋の連休などにも頻繁に帰郷しては、山の暮らしになじんできました。春の山菜や秋の茸も、採れれば早速孫たちに送りました。定年になったら福島に帰ると言って、家を建てる場所まで選定していた子供もいました。今回の原発事故は、ふるさとの地に住む老夫婦の残りの人生を踏みにじってしまったばかりでなく、子供たちや孫たちのふるさとまでも、根こそぎ奪い取ってしまったのです。

「小島君と言う人はいるか？」
　私が勤めていた郵便局の窓口に、事務室一杯にひびき渡るような大声で訪ねてきたずんぐり小太りの男が、双葉町議会議員の岩本忠夫でありました。当時私は二十代半ば、山の中の小さな郵便局の窓口係をしていました。色黒・ギョロ眼の岩本は、初対面である私に、「この双葉郡に、郡内全域に及ぶ運動体として、［憲法を守る会］という組織を作りたい。中身は原発反対運動を中心に活動したいので、手伝ってほしい」と熱っぽく呼びかけました。それから準備運動を始め組織化に着手し、委員長・岩本忠夫、事務局長・私というメンバーでスタートしたのですが、この組織が双葉地方における原発反対運動の草分けとなりました。反原発運動でありながら、会の名称をカムフラージュするところに、双葉郡のむずかしい地域事情があったと思います。

When we set up the organization, the first Fukushima Nuclear Power Plant was already under construction between the towns of Okuma and Futaba. Then, Tokyo Electric Power Company started to look for a site for the second plant between the towns of Tomioka and Naraha. They were going to buy the site from landowners. We had to hurry to organize an anti-nuclear movement not to repeat the mistake of allowing the construction of the first Fukushima Nuclear Power Plant. We joined the landowners who didn't wish to sell their farmland in Tomioka and Naraha. A fierce battle took place over the pros and cons of nuclear power plants, which divided the town into two. I visited landowners and participated in the meetings. Night after night I rode my motorbike more than 30 kilometers to join them. In the end, we lost and let the company construct the second Fukushima Nuclear Power Plant. However, the movement spread all over Futaba County and has persisted until present.

I lived in an area which is 25 kilometers away from the first Fukushima Nuclear Power Plant. Our village consisted of fewer than 500 households, located in a mountain valley, which forms the watershed of the Pacific Ocean side of the Abukuma mountains and Abukuma River basin. Since the sites of the nuclear power plants do not directly belong to our village, we got very little nuclear power subsidies, or "Nuclear Power Grants." Yet once the accident occurred, every city, town and village suffered from it, whether directly or indirectly. Both residents who opposed the nuclear power and those who were for it had to suffer from it. Residents have no choice but to be victims regardless of the pros and cons. The fact is that all residents are the victim and the government and Tokyo Electric Power Company are the assailant. We should keep that in

私たちが立ち上がったその当時は、大熊・双葉両町にまたがる福島第一原発が、すでに建設着工されており、引き続き東電は富岡・楢葉両町に、福島第二原発を建設すべく、土地買収に動いていた。私たちは第一原発の轍を踏まないために、早急に建設反対の火の手を上げなければならない。農地を手離したくない富岡町・楢葉町の地権者と手を組んで、町を二分する熾烈なたたかいが展開されました。私も毎晩々々片道三十数キロの道をバイクで往復し、地権者の家を訪問したり会議に参加したりしていました。結果としては戦いに敗れ、第二原発の着工を許しはしたものの、その運動は双葉郡全体に広がり、今に引き継がれています。

　私が住んでいた地域は、原発から直線距離で25キロ程の地点にあります。阿武隈山脈の太平洋側と阿武隈川流域の分水嶺にあたる山間に、集落が散在する、世帯数五百戸足らずの村です。直接原発立地村ではないため、俗に原発マネーといわれる交付金も、おこぼれ程度しか廻ってこなかった、山間僻地の小村です。しかし一旦事故が起きてしまえば、直接立地町村であれ、周辺町村であれ、その被害だけは全地域に及び、原発に反対した人も賛成した人も、共に等しく被災者となる。住民は反対も賛成も関係なく、否応なしに被害者にされてしまうのです。つまり今の状況は、被害者である全住民と、加害者である政府・東京電力が明確に分離・対立している。この関係、この構図を、正しくとらえる必要があると考えています。

mind and never forget it.

I was exiled from my home in Tokyo by the war and again ousted from my second home by this nuclear accident. In my mind war and nuclear power are closely related to each other. Carrying out the war was the primary national preoccupation of the government during WW II and so has been the promotion of nuclear power plants after the war.

The war encouraged people to fight in the battlefield. It endangered the lives of people by air raids, ground battles in Okinawa, and atomic bombs. Likewise nuclear power plants put lives at risk. The nuclear accident made that clear.

Over the course of the nuclear power accident, people referred to the public announcements by the Japanese government as "News from the Headquarters of the Imperial Army," that is, lies. They concealed the results of simulations by SPEEDI[7]. Consequently, people in Namie were evacuated to the northern part of the town, which in fact had the highest radiation levels of the area. Villagers in Iidate were left for more than a month in a district that was highly contaminated by radioactivity. The government did not let them know this fact. How does this affect their lives? The government knew they were in danger but neglected to publicize it; they treated those people as "the deserted." It proved that the national policy of promoting nuclear power was based on deserting people during an emergency.

In the case of the nuclear accident in Fukushima, there is very little difference from war time in that the government didn't hesitate to control and manipulate information. Moreover, we should remember

---

7 SPEEDI: System for Prediction of Environmental Emergency Dose Information

戦争でふるさと・東京を追われ、原発事故でもう一度「第二のふるさと」から追い出される。そうした経験から私の記憶の中では、戦争と原発がいつも一直線に結びつきます。戦争の遂行が時の政府の唯一の国策であるように、原発建設の推進も国策として強行されました。戦争が国民を戦地に駆り出して生命を捨てさせる。あるいは国民の命を空襲や沖縄戦、原爆投下などの危険にさらすのと同じように、原発も又国民を生命の危険に直面させるという事実を、今回の原発事故が明らかにしました。

　原発事故のさ中、公表される政府の報告は、「大本営発表」と言われ続けた。「ＳＰＥＥＤＩ」のシュミレーション隠蔽によって、最も放射線量の高い浪江町北西部に、何も知らされずに避難させられた浪江町民や、事実を伏せられたまま高濃度の汚染地区に、一か月以上も放置された飯舘の村民は、これから先どう生きてゆけばいいのでしょうか。こうした政府の確信犯的対応は、まさに国民を切り捨てるという意味での、「棄民」と言う以外ありません。それは国策と称して推進を図って来た原発政策そのものが、「棄民」という土台の上に成り立っていることを、受け止めるべき証しでもあります。

　こうして情報の統制・操作が平然と進められたことは、戦争の時代と少しも変りがない。そして更に戦争の遂行も原発

the national policies of carrying out war and promoting nuclear power, are similar in that people are neglected at the cost of their invaluable lives. After the war, Japan adopted the "Peace Constitution," and became a member of democratic society. Yet it is only democracy on paper. Couldn't it be said that this nuclear accident made it clear that Japanese politics, economy and social structure has not changed since WW II?

Since I evacuated my home and have been living in Tokyo, I left almost all my records of the anti-nuclear movement at home. If my memory is correct, I was involved in the establishment of "The Association for Protecting the Constitution" for about 3 or 4 years. Then it developed into "The Anti-Nuclear Power Alliance," officially changing its name. When I had to concentrate on the workers' movement, I passed the baton of the anti-nuclear movement on to newer activists.

I worked for a post office and belonged to "Zentei" (All Workers' Union for the Postal Service.). So I became an executive member of the union in Futaba branch and then in its Fukushima branch. At that time, Tokyo Electric Power Company strengthened its influence over the district.

Under the guidance of the prefectural and national governments, the local government made residents agree to nuclear power. Activists against nuclear power were being isolated and were split from one another. Mr. Iwamoto Tadao, who once had been elected a member of the prefectural assembly, failed in the election again and again. He later became to be pro-nuclear power when he ran for the mayoral election in Futaba town.

推進も、国策のためには国民の生命を犠牲にしてはばからないという冷酷な思想が、その根底にあることを忘れてはならないと考えます。戦後日本は平和憲法を持ち、民主主義国の仲間入りをしたと言われます。しかし形の上では民主主義であっても、日本の政治・経済、そして社会のありようは、戦争の時代とどこも変らないという事実を、突きつけられたのが今回の原発事故ではなかったでしょうか。

　今東京で避難生活をしている身で、手元に当時を振り返る資料もありませんが、「憲法を守る会」の活動にたずさわった時期は、多分三～四年位だったかと思います。その後「憲法を守る会」を正式に「原発反対同盟」と改称するなどに発展するのですが、私は地域活動を後輩にバトンタッチし、労働運動に専念しなければならない事情が生じました。
　職場が郵便局なので、労働組合は全逓信労働組合（通称全逓）で、その組織で双葉支部や福島地区本部などの役員を務めることとなりました。その頃東電の地域支配が更に強化され、自治体は国・県の指導のもとに住民への圧力を強めて、活動家の切り崩し・孤立化などが進められました。一度は県議会議員に当選した岩本忠夫が、その後何度も落選をするなどの経過があって、双葉町長選に立候補する段階で、東京電力の圧力に屈し、原発容認に回るという一幕もありました。
　私は全逓の青年部で活動していた時期から音楽活動にかかわって来た経緯もあり、全逓本部が全国組織の運動体として、「全逓全国音楽協議会」を結成することとなったため、準備

I have been involved in music since I became a member of the Youth Division of Zentei. When the Zentei organized the "All Unions Music Association of Zentei," I helped the organization committee and was elected to be the first president. I worked at it for ten years. "The All Unions Music Association of Zentei" belongs to the "Nihon Music Association." Therefore, I also took part in the foundation of a Fukushima branch. Through my activities, I aimed to express my opinion against nuclear power in music and to propagate the anti-nuclear power movement.

As for my "Works Three Decades Ago," they were written as poetry for several musical festivals. The first poem, "Workers for Subcontractors at a Nuclear Power Plant," was requested as a leading poem in "The Annual of the Japan Congress against Atomic Bombs and Hydrogen Bombs" in 1980 and it was published that year. From then on I continued to compose poems for eight years, though I was not sure that my poems could be called poetry. I had so much to say that I just wrote them. I am indebted to Jyugatsu-sha publishers for letting me write poems freely without any limit on lines or word count. I am deeply grateful to Mr. Otsuki Shigenobu, then the representative of the publishers, who collected the missing works of mine when I published my book.

Moreover, I would like to thank many people who helped me in publishing this book. My daughter, Sakaguchi Mika, encouraged me to publish it as a 'compatriot' when I was reluctant to do so at first. She asked Ms. Oyama Misako, an editor with whom she had been acquainted, whether my draft was appropriate to publish. My draft, then, was sent to Mr. Kamata Satoshi, a writer and was handed to Mr. Hidaka Norimichi, an old friend of his and the representative of

活動からこれにたずさわって、初代会長に選ばれ、十期（十年）を務めました。「全遍音協」（通称）は日本音楽協議会にも所属していたので、日音協福島県支部の結成にも関わり、その中で「原発反対」の意識を音楽で表現し、広めて行こうという目標を掲げて、活動してきました。

　「三十年前の作品」群は、その時期構成詩として各種音楽祭などで発表されたもので、最初の「原発下請労働者」は、当時原水禁運動の経過を年鑑として発行されていた「（一九）80原水禁」に、巻頭詩として掲載するよう求められました。当時私は言いたいことが山ほどあるという気持でもあったため、詩という範疇に属するのかどうかは別として、以降八年間書き続けました。何の制約もなく行数無制限で書かせてくれた「十月社」に、感謝する以外ありません。また今回この作品群を収録するに当たって、私自身は散逸して手元にない部分もあったのですが、これをまとめてくださった当時の代表大槻重信氏に深く感謝を申し上げたい。

　本書刊行に至るまで多くの方々の縁をいただいた。娘・坂口美日は、公刊をためらう私に「同志」としての立場で刊行をうながし、知己を得た編集者の大山美佐子さんの判断を仰いだ。そしてゆくりなくも原稿は大山さんから鎌田慧さんに届けられ、鎌田さん旧知の西田書店・日高徳迪さんの手に渡った。私はいま、それぞれの方々もまた「同志」との思いを深くする。推薦文を寄せていただいた石川逸子さん、現在避

Nishida Shoten Publishing Company. I was deeply thankful for those 'compatriots.' I would like to express my sincere gratitude to Ms. Ishikawa Itsuko, a poet who contributed a recommendation and to Mr. Murakami Morimasa, Mayor of Musashino, Tokyo where I live my evacuee life.

March 6, 2013
Kojima Chikara

難生活をしている地元の武蔵野市長・邑上守正さんもまた然りであり、心からの謝意を申し上げる次第です。
　　　　二〇一三年三月六日
　　　　　　　　　　　　　　　　　　　小　島　　力

Translator's Afterword

It was spring in 2013 when a friend of mine gave me a Japanese poetry book titled, "Waga Namida Boubou," which means "My Tears Flow Endlessly." It was a book written by his brother who was a victim of the nuclear accident in Fukushima. He said that his brother, Mr. Kojima Chikara was living as evacuee in Tokyo. After reading this book, I was very much impressed not only by each poem protesting against the unfairness of nuclear power, but also by the author's way of life. Mr. Kojima, had long been an activist against nuclear power, a labor unionist, an organizer for workers' music festivals, and a poet, all while he was working at a post office. I introduced his poetry to the members of my reading group in the summer of 2013. A year later, I invited Mr. Kojima to an event called "Komae Peace Festival," organized every August in Komae, Tokyo, where I live. He recited a few poems from his book and gave a speech titled "Katsurao Village Now: All Villagers Had to Be Evacuated from the Fukushima Nuclear Power Accident."

It was my wish that others could read his poems, and that inspired me to translate this poetry book into English. Nuclear power influences virtually every citizen on earth and their offspring. This is the reason I decided to publish this bilingual poetry book.

In his speech in Komae, Mr. Kojima criticized the present system of compensation for the damage caused by the nuclear accident. Each victim must claim compensation using a form prepared by the

訳者あとがき

　福島の原発事故から二年たった2013年の春、私は知人から「原発事故で東京に避難している兄が書いたものです。」と一冊の詩集を贈られた。その詩集『わが涙滂々』を読んで、原発の理不尽さを訴える一つ一つの詩のすばらしさと共に、働きながら長年、原発反対運動、労働運動、音楽活動に取り組み、詩を書き続けてこられた著者小島力さんの真摯な生き方に感銘を受けた。早速その夏に私の読書会の仲間に、この詩集を紹介し、また翌年に、私の住む東京都狛江市で毎年八月に実施している「こまえ平和フェスタ」という催しに小島力さんを講演者としてお招きした。彼はこの詩集の幾つかの詩を朗読し、「福島原発事故で全村避難・葛尾村の今」の題でお話しされた。
　私の周囲だけでなく、さらにもっと多くの人々に彼の詩を読んで欲しいと思いこの本を英訳することにした。なぜなら原発の問題は、日本のみならず世界のすべての国に住む人々とその子孫の生命に関わることだからである。

　「こまえ平和フェスタ」での講演で小島力さんは被災者の立場から、原発事故の賠償の現状に疑問を呈した。被災者個人が一人ひとりで加害者側の東京電力が作成した用紙で賠償

perpetrator, Tokyo Electric Power Company (TEPCO). It is TEPCO that decides the appropriate compensation for the claim according to its own standards. TEPCO now offers compensation of 100,000 yen a month for each victim for psychological damage, and must pay more for real estate and movable belongings. In August 2011, a new law on compensation for nuclear damage was enacted and a new compensation agency was established. TEPCO has benefited from the law. This is because damage from nuclear accidents is actually compensated for by taxes paid by the Japanese people and by increases in electricity charges. Therefore, TEPCO and the government have become less responsible for the accident. In September 2011, the government established an Alternative Dispute Resolution Center (ADR) on compensation for nuclear damage. Mr. Kojima with other victims in Katsurao village, began preparing for a collective claim to the Center. They thought it would ameliorate the humiliating system of government and TEPCO vs. individual victims. In January 2013 Mr. Kojima, his wife and other victims organized themselves into the Association to Advance the Collective Claim for Compensation in Katsurao Village. He has been a representative of the association ever since.

In his speech, Mr. Kojima criticized the methods for decontamination of radioactivity and the revisions in the area of designated evacuation zones. The government only decontaminates 20 meters around houses and along roads and rivers. The government does not decontaminate forests and inhabited lands, which make up the majority of Katsurao village. Therefore, so called "hot spots," which are highly contaminated, continue to pollute the village here and

請求をし、また東京電力が定めた基準に基づきそれが査定されることは不当であると言っている。現在東電が避難者に支払う精神的損害への賠償である慰謝料は、一人当たり月額10万円であるが、土地、建物や家財などへの損害賠償は個別に請求することになっている。2011年8月、「原子力損害賠償支援機構法」[1]が制定され、東京電力は機構から賠償の資金援助をうけることになった。最終的に原発事故の賠償金は、国民の税金や電気料金値上げによって支払うことになる。この仕組みでは加害者の東京電力と原発を推進してきた政府の責任があいまいになってしまうと彼は指摘する。小島力さんは葛尾村の被災者たちと共に、2011年9月に設立された公的機関「原子力損害賠償紛争解決センター（ADR）」に対して、集団申立をする運動を進めている。そうすれば、少なくとも「政府・東京電力　対　被災者一個人」という屈辱的な構図から脱却できるのではないかと考えたからである。彼は妻と二人で、2012年に集団申立の呼びかけ人になり、発起人、賛同者たちと共に2013年1月「葛尾村原発賠償集団申立推進会」を結成した。彼は現在その代表となっている。

　講演で彼は、除染と避難区域見直しの問題点も指摘された。除染は家の周囲20ｍ、道路、河川の両脇20ｍとなっているが、葛尾村の大部分を占める山林、原野は手つかずのままである。その結果、除染が終わってもまだ高濃度の汚染箇所が散在し

1　現在は、改正され「原子力損害賠償・廃炉等支援機構法」

there. The government has spent 60 billion yen on the decontamination of Katsurao village so far. Mr. Kojima strongly doubts the effectiveness of the decontamination itself. Moreover, he is very apprehensive and angry about the government move to change the minimum level of radioactive exposure acceptable for people to return. The objective of the decontamination was originally to lower the exposure level to under 1 milli Sv a year. Yet they have not been able to achieve that level yet. Then the government changed the minimum level from 1 to 20 milli Sv. The government was planning to revise the evacuation zones and to urge evacuees to return. He is very critical of the government and its policies that abandon people. Mr. Kojima, at the end of his speech, talked about the future of the victims of nuclear accidents. He said, "We will only be able to have hope when the majority of Japanese are against the utilization of nuclear power and in favor of asking for appropriate reparation to the victims rather than helping TEPCO."

Over five years have passed since the Fukushima nuclear accident caused by the earthquake and tsunami in 2011. In Fukushima prefecture, there are six towns and villages, including Katsurao village, where many residents cannot go back home. The number of people who have evacuated from Fukushima now is said to exceed 100,000. Was this an accident that caused by earthquake and tsunami "beyond prediction?" Was it a "once-in-a-thousand year" outlier? It was indeed an unprecedented accident, but it comes down to human negligence. It was obviously not a natural disaster. In order not to have another nuclear accident again, all we can do is to clarify the cause of the accident and to spread the anti-nuclear power movement

ている。葛尾村だけでも600億円という莫大な費用をかけた除染そのものの有効性に疑問を持つという。また除染終了を根拠に政府が避難指示を解除しようとすることに強い危惧と怒りを感じている。政府は除染で年間被曝量１ミリSv以下という目標が達成できないとわかると、それを一気に20ミリSvに引き上げて帰還を迫ることにした。これはまさに被災者切り捨ての、棄民政策であると小島さんは断じている。小島力さんは、講演の最後に原発被災者の未来は、多くの国民が「原発の再稼働をくい止め」「東電救済より被災者にまともな補償、賠償を」という確固たる声を挙げるときに見えてくるという希望の言葉で締めくくられた。

　2011年の東日本大震災によって引き起こされた福島の原発事故からまもなく５年以上経つが、福島県の被災地では、今でも葛尾村を含む６町村では多くの住民は故郷に帰れずに避難先で暮らしている。福島の原発事故で故郷を離れた人の数は全体で十万人を超えるとも言われている。福島の原発事故は、「千年に一度」の大地震と大津波によってもたらされた「想定外」の事故という認識でよいのだろうか。それが人災でもあったという視点を持たなければならないのではないだろうか。このような原発事故を再び起こさない為に、私たちができることは、被災者の苦悩に目を向けながら、事故の真相を知り多くの人々にそれを伝え、原発再稼働反対の世論を作っていくことではないだろうか。

while sympathizing with the victims of the accident.

As for the publication of this book, I am very grateful to the following people for working on it. Firstly, I would like to express my heartfelt gratitude to Mr. Kojima Chikara, the author of the original book. He was kind enough to give me permission to translate two chapters out of three in his book into English and answered all the questions I had in my translation work. Secondly, I am deeply indebted to Mr. Hidaka Norimichi, a representative of the Nishida Publishing Company. He was very helpful and gave me many useful ideas about publishing this book. Lastly, I would like to thank Mr. Alex Heard from Australia and Ms. Lorinda Kiyama from the United States, who proofread my English translation draft consulting the original poetry book in Japanese, and gave me helpful guidance in translation.

Written 30 years after the Chernobyl nuclear accident
and five years after the Fukushima nuclear accident.

November 2016
Noda Setsuko

この本の出版に際して、私は次の方々に大変お世話になり厚くお礼を申し上げたい。最初に、この詩集の原作者である小島力さんに心から感謝したい。彼は詩集の三つの章から二つを英訳したいという私の提案を快く許可してくださり、また詩集の中の言葉づかいに関する質問に丁寧に答えてくださった。また出版には西田書店の代表の日高徳迪さんに大変お世話になった。全く知識のない私に、彼は出版に関して多くの有益な助言と教えを与えてくださった。最後に私の英訳原稿の校正を担当したオーストラリア出身のアレックスハードさんとアメリカ出身の木山ロリンダさんにお礼を申し上げたい。二人には日本語の詩集を参照しながら私の英訳原稿を校正していただいた。

チェルノブイリ原発事故から30年目、
福島原発事故から5年目に

2016年11月

野田説子

詩集わが涙滂々（抄）
原発にふるさとを追われて
A Selection of Poetry Works:
MY TEARS FLOW ENDLESSLY
Forcrd Out of House and Home
by the Fukushima Nuclear Power Accident

2017年3月6日初版第1刷発行
2018年6月20日初版第2刷発行

著 者	小島　力	Chikara Kojima
訳 者	野田説子	Setsuko Noda
発行者	日高徳迪	Norimichi Hidaka
装 丁	桂川　潤	Jun Katsuragawa

発行所　西田書店　Nishida-syoten
東京都千代田区神田神保町2-34 山本ビル
Tel 03-3261-4509 Fax 03-3262-4643
http://www.nishida-shoten.co.jp

ISBN978-4-88866-612-1
Ⓒ 2017　Chikara Kojima & Setsuko Noda　Printed in Japan
＊定価は表紙に提示してあります。